Me, Love
and Johnny King

A Tale of Love, Tobacco and
Tranmere Rovers

Me, Love
and Johnny King

A Tale of Love, Tobacco and
Tranmere Rovers

Thomas P. Moffatt

Winchester, UK
Washington, USA

First published by Roundfire Books, 2013
Roundfire Books is an imprint of John Hunt Publishing Ltd., Laurel House, Station Approach,
Alresford, Hants, SO24 9JH, UK
office1@jhpbooks.net
www.johnhuntpublishing.com
www.roundfire-books.com

For distributor details and how to order please visit the 'Ordering' section on our website.

Text copyright: Thomas P. Moffatt 2012

ISBN: 978 1 78099 687 5

Design: Stuart Davies

Printed and bound by CPI Group (UK) Ltd, Croydon, CR0 4YY

We operate a distinctive and ethical publishing philosophy in all
areas of our business, from our global network of authors to
production and worldwide distribution.

CONTENTS

CHAPTER ONE

Welcome to Rock Ferry

Rock Ferry is a strange place. I've lived in this area of Birkenhead for almost all my life and it never fails to shock me. For example the pub up the road by the station, I've been going in there on a semi-regular basis since I was 16. I live locally and I know most of the people in there but I can walk in at any given time of the day during opening hours and I'll be given a questioning look by the natives as if to say, "Are you local? What are you doing in here? This is local pub for local people!" It's like something out of *The League of Gentleman,* a place inhabited by a group of increasingly bizarre and unbelievable people. It never fails to amaze me; there's people who go in there who've known me since I was a little kid, and the moment I walk in and sit down for a drink they pretend they don't know me, then when I order a pint of lager they stare at me as if I'd asked for a pint of human blood and packet of deep-fried baby brains then attempted to start a conversation about how great the Yorkshire Ripper was or even worse how great Margaret Thatcher was. I've never been made to feel welcome in there.

There's this bloke who lives on the road where my gran used to live; he's known me since I was knee high. Whenever I went to my grandmother's he would always say hello and even now should I bump into him in the street he always says, "Hello, Tommy!" and stops for a chat. Nice enough bloke you're probably thinking; he is except he drinks in that pub by the station. Should I wander into that pub by the station when he's having a pint then he's never met me before in his life and hasn't a clue who Tommy is. Some people, eh?

I remember when I was about 19, me and a couple of mates went in there for a few scoops and couple of games of darts, within minutes of throwing our last dart every regular in the pub lined up in a queue to throw a few darts. Men who had last thrown a dart when James Callaghan was Prime Minister got up to chuck a few arrows to make it clear to a group of teenagers they weren't welcome in their pub. One dart, two darts, a cold stare in our direction...then they would throw the third dart. They stood at the oche commenting on how they didn't like kids in their pub on their dartboard, how teenagers' behaviour is no place for the pub and that it was a place for grown-ups. Had I been older and wiser I might have asked – who are the real grown-ups around here? Whose behaviour really is childish; those having a quiet drink or the fools flapping their gums?

A night out in Rock Ferry is something to behold; you'll either have one of the greatest nights of your life or one of the worst. There's no middle ground, you'll be with your best mates or complete tossers, and you'll either meet the greatest girl in the world or suffer a dose of the Kermits and be stalked by some demented pig. On a night out in Rock Ferry the drink will either flow like the proverbial amber nectar or be as rank as stagnant ditch water, some nights you'll be able to sink 20 pints and feel nothing, on other nights you will be chucking up after three. When you go home you'll either flag down the first cab you see or you'll be helped home by the local constabulary via a night at that well-known hostelry, the Nick.

Probably the strangest phenomenon to be encountered in Rock Ferry is what I like to call 'Rock Ferry Tobacco Duty'. Walk along Bedford Road on any given Saturday smoking a ciggie when the Rovers are playing at home and a chirpy native will walk up, take note of your Tranmere Rovers shirt and/or scarf and ask, "Who are you playing today, mate?" You'll reply with the appropriate opposition to which your chirpy acquaintance will reply along the lines of, "Oh, bit of a toughie that one!" or "That will be three points in the bag!" depending on the reputation of the opposition. Then it comes; after a pause your acquaintance will ask, "Have you got a spare ciggie...? And do you have a spare one for later?"

I don't know what gets me most about Rock Ferry Tobacco Duty – the bare-faced cheek of walking up to someone you don't know on a false pretence just to ask for a cigarette and one for later or living less than 10 minutes away from your local league club and not knowing who they're playing. I wouldn't mind but they all seem to be wearing a Liverpool or Everton shirt! Or on some occasions, Manchester Bloody United! Sorry, I shouldn't swear! How rude of me – I should say That Bloody Stretford Mob!

Speaking of That Bloody Stretford Mob, glory hunters have always done my head in. For those of you who don't know what a glory hunter is they are one of those irritating people who supports a football or sports team simply because they are winning or have a championship to make themselves look like winners and then switch allegiance at any given opportunity, most likely when someone else takes over in the dominant position. Glory hunters often attach themselves to teams such as That Bloody Stretford Mob because they win their fair share of trophies. A lot of them are silly little teenage girls who fancy a certain player and haven't got the foggiest about the game itself. Then again there are men who are like that, too.

When I was at school back in the days when *Mr Blobby* was top of the charts, Accrington Stanley were just a faded pop-culture reference in a milk advert and the Internet was still just a thing for the pale, geeky and friendless, we had this annoying kid in our form, he was a Man United fan. Or so he said. He supported Leeds United for a year and then Blackburn Rovers for a season and nearly became a Newcastle United fan. He had a shirt bought ready until Kevin Keegan did his infamous "I'll love it" speech and the rest was history; it didn't all end in disaster for the annoying kid, he kept the receipt so he was able to get his money refunded and go back to supporting That

Bloody Stretford Mob. He was a glory hunter in every sense. He supported whoever was champ in whatever sport that was in the spotlight at the time. Before the 1994 World Cup he told everyone that his favourites Germany would win; after the 1994 World Cup he was the world's biggest Brazil fan. I became sick and tired of hearing about Wigan Rugby League club and how great the golfer Nick Faldo was when he won (and only when he won!). After the 1992 Olympics he bleated endlessly about his newfound hero Linford Christie and how he himself was now in training to become the next Christie. The worst was when Wimbledon came around, all we would hear was tennis, tennis and more flipping tennis. I hate tennis; I would go out of my way to avoid tennis; I guess it would be toss-up between tennis and That Bloody Stretford Mob in the universal contest of what I hate most. The only good thing was that Wimbledon was on for only two weeks a year and not 52 weeks. I guess That Bloody Stretford Mob comes out top in that contest.

I've never glory-hunted; I've been accused of it when my team, Tranmere Rovers, are in the spotlight but it's one thing I don't do – I always back the underdog unless they are a fluky chinless wonder or taking on the Rovers. I've always felt pity for glory hunters, so emotionally insecure that they need everyone to believe they support the best so they attach themselves to the champions because it makes them look like a champion. So unbelievably shallow they need people to believe they support the best. They probably hold a low-paid, unskilled job, have a partner who was amongst the dregs at the bottom of the barrel and live somewhere lousy. Or they are insecure in their jobs, can't find anyone to go out with them and still live with their parents.

I'm Birkenhead born and bred and ever since I was a kid my team has been (as I mentioned before) Tranmere Rovers, the Super Whites and I was a member of the tribe known as the Super White Army. I still remember the first time I went to Prenton Park. I was six years old; it was a freezing cold Friday evening. I sat on my granddad's shoulders, the smoke from his Woodbines wafting up my nose. A group of lads from the Isle of Man Steam Packet Company stood nearby having walked up from the docks earlier that evening having been given a subsidy to attend. It was the days of terraced stands and dodgy meat pies at half-time; "Couldn't find better in Birkenhead, Tommy lad!" said my granddad as we tucked in at half-time, "What have you been eating, Tommy?!" shrieked my mother when I threw up during the middle of the night. That was the night I lost my Prenton virginity and we beat Exeter City two nil. Well, I think we did.

From then on every time I could, I would go to Prenton. Back then I was always a well-behaved little boy, I worked it out early in life that if I was good, helped my parents and grandparents the more I'd go to see my beloved Tranmere. Birthdays and Christmases were easy for my family, a ticket to Prenton for the next home game. I always made sure I drank plenty of milk, too, because if I didn't when I grew up I'd only be good enough to play for Accrington Stanley! As I got older I would get to home and away games by working little jobs for money such as mowing lawns, tidying gardens, fetching shopping. As a teenager I got a job scrubbing dishes in a Chinese restaurant just to get me to Prenton Park on a regular basis. One Saturday afternoon I cycled all the way to Stoke to watch John Aldridge score a hat-trick against Port Vale; my family didn't know where I was and I got the biggest bollocking of my life when I got in just after midnight as apparently my mother was just about to phone the police but, hey, it was worth it despite being grounded for a fortnight. I did my training at the Wirral Metropolitan College and the bulk of my money I got for my training allowance went to seeing the Rovers. I gained my qualification and eventually set up my own business. That's when the hard work paid off and eventually I was able to afford a season ticket in the Johnny King Stand.

Johnny King, what a man! It was his time as our manager that inspired and cultivated my love for all things super and white from Birkenhead. He took the Rovers from the bowels of the football league where we faced a potential future in the despairing loneliness of the non-leagues to the brink of the Promised Land which was the Premiership. He saw us through good and bad, thick and thin, triumph and heartbreak. The legend that is Johnny King still lives on at Prenton Park; when the Borough Road stand was redeveloped who would be more fitting for the stand to be named after than the great Johnny King.

My relationship with Tranmere felt like one of life and history's great love affairs. The cup runs under John Aldridge that saw us reach two FA Cup quarter finals and one League Cup final; crashing out of the play-offs under the great Mr King; the frustration of the 1994 League Cup semi versus Villa; promotion from the old Fourth Division; the luck of the 1990 promotion (thank you, Swindon!); relegation under John Aldridge; St Yates Day (known to the common football fan as the 27th January) when Steve Yates scored two goals when we beat Everton 3-0 in the fourth round of the Cup in 2001 – Tranmere had the ability to either break my heart or make me feel like I was the King of the World! They brought every emotion possible out in me; I lost girlfriends who believed I thought more of my team than them, "you'd rather be at that football ground than with us, Tommy!" many of them had told me; Tranmere Rovers were the love of my life and as far as I was concerned I believed that only fools falls in love; Tranmere Rovers were my one true love and as far as I was concerned there could be no other I could truly love more than the Rovers. But I was wrong, so very wrong...

"And who the flip is Lincoln Davies?" I asked, without the slightest clue in the world to what I had just been told.

It was the third round of the Cup and we were at home to York City. The program told us that one to watch for York City was Lincoln Davies. I was stood by my seat in the Johnny King Stand, my old pal 'Sid' said that this young chap Lincoln Davies had a bright future by all accounts, well he told me it said so in the program. It still led me to retort, "Who the flip is Lincoln Davies?" although I believe that flip wasn't the adjective I used.

"He's a Barbadian international, apparently Wigan Athletic and a few others in the top flight have shown interest in him," said a heavenly voice to my left.

Slowly I looked to my left and two seats away was the most beautiful girl in the world. Our eyes met, we both smiled, "I hope that's answered your question," she said.

"Yes, it has," I replied with a slight stammer; that moment when I first saw her it was if time stood still, I was somewhat captivated by her beauty. Everything around her seemed to cloud over and continue in slow motion.

She smiled a beautiful smile. It was a sunny January afternoon, the type we get in the first few weeks of January to taunt us before we get the worst of the winter weather. The sun shone on her lovely long brown hair which rested over her Tranmere scarf; all I could do was gaze at her beautiful smile and gorgeous eyes; this girl was the most beautiful woman I had ever seen in my life!

"I'm Katie," she said offering a handshake.

"Hi Katie, I'm Tommy," I said nervously whilst shaking her hand. "That's Sid," I added pointing to Sid.

"How do, love!" chirped Sid with a cheerful wave, Katie waved back.

For the next 20 minutes we kept exchanging glances and smiles; for the first time in over two decades I was at Prenton Park on match day watching Tranmere Rovers and the football wasn't the main thing on my mind; there was a ringing in my ears and a pounding in my heart. She was gorgeous. I've never seen a Tranmere shirt look so good. Something told me this was love at first sight and I couldn't believe it; straight away something deep down told me she was the one. Had this fool fallen in love? I had to break the ice – easier said than done! After twenty minutes of wondering what to do or say with the most beautiful woman I had had ever seen in my life, I finally spoke, "So do you come here regularly, Katie?" I asked, nervously.

"When I can, what about you?" she replied

"I'm a season-ticket holder!" I informed her, proudly.

"Something I've always wanted!" Katie told me. "I can't afford it on my salary!"

"I haven't seen you in the Johnny King Stand before!" I said to Katie

"I always used to sit in the Main Stand," Katie informed me, "but someone told me it was cheaper in the Johnny King Stand!"

"Not by much," I replied. "Only by about a quid! I prefer it here because you're closer to the touchline!"

She smiled her beautiful smile; I smiled at her, she looked so beautiful with the setting sun's rays shining on her hair, her lovely eyes and that smile of hers that just wanted to make me walk over and kiss her like some suave James Bond type in a Hollywood movie.

"I think you're in there, Tommy!" whispered Sid.

"Don't be daft!" I whispered back.

"Go on!" he urged. "She's stunning!"

I'd known Sid for years; he had been best friends with my Old Man and his brother Billy; in many ways Sid was like a surrogate uncle to me. Sid was without a shadow of a doubt one of the biggest characters you could ever meet. A man who had football and Tranmere pumping through his veins, a man who, you will learn, threw many stereotypes out of the window but held on to a few at the same time. However, if you need any fact, any stat, Sid was your man. His name wasn't really Sid; in fact I don't know what his name was, I always knew him simply as Sid. People said he was just known as Sid because he spoke with a hiss in his voice.

"She's a very attractive girl!" hissed Sid.

"I know!" I said, nervously.

"Then talk to her!" he urged. "It's easy!"

"What would you know about talking to girls?" I asked dryly.

Before Sid could reply Alan Mahon put the ball into the box and Ian Thomas-Moore slotted it home; we all rose to our feet to celebrate because the Rovers were one nil ahead, "He finished that well!" I said to Katie.

"It was okay, I've seen better!" she said with a smile. I laughed, she laughed. "You're nice!" she added, suddenly gazing into my eyes.

"So are you!" I said looking her in the eyes; we looked at each other and smiled again. If I could go back in time and be there again right at that moment I would have run on to the pitch and kissed Ian Thomas-Moore; if it wasn't for his goal we wouldn't have spoken and it would never have begun. Mind you, if I ran on to the pitch I would have been escorted home via that hostelry known as the Nick by Mr Policeman! Thankfully the secrets of time travel have not been discovered so that's not a possibility; yet.

I've always felt that smiling is so important; when you smile at somebody it can set the whole tone for things to come, it's a great relaxant to the whole atmosphere. It can say more than any tacky chat-up line; a beautiful smile is so vital for me. Most importantly Katie had one.

I felt a connection straight away for this beautiful girl. I may have bleated on about it but she was simply amazing. For the rest of the game we analysed each individual player's game, Tranmere good – York bad; we commentated on the shots, the saves, the nearly moments; Sid performing his party trick by spilling his half-time coffee; a hissy fit from a York player; those bad shots that miss the goal by a country mile and instantly bring the cult figure of Jason Lee to mind; the ref getting hit in the back of the head by the ball. We had a laugh that afternoon. I felt a vital spark. She ticked all my boxes: lovely eyes, gorgeous smile, long brown hair, she supported Tranmere and looked so great in her Tranmere shirt.

It was deep into the second half when Thomas-Moore had added a second with a volley from the penalty spot before Chris Shuker had slotted home from a tight angle. We were 3-0 up and although York had put up a fair scrap we had overcome them; we were now home and dry and our name would be in the draw for the fourth round of the Cup on Sunday.

"What are you doing after the game, Katie?" I enquired, my nerves jangling with a mixture of hope and fear.

"I'll probably go home," she replied.

"Would you like a drink in the Prenton Park?" I asked hopefully.

"I'm a bit skint," she told me.

"I'll buy you a couple," I offered.

"I don't really know you, Tommy!" Katie answered.

"That's not a problem," I began. "I want to get to know you..."

"Okay, that'd be lovely!" she said with a smile.

Four minutes of overtime came then went and the final whistle sounded. Five minutes later I was in the Prenton Park Pub ordering two pints of lager and two minutes after that we began our first conversation. I told Katie of my first visit to Prenton Park sat on my grandfather's shoulders; I recalled other visits including the first game I had met Sid; the Isle of Man Steam Packet boys who got a concession on a Friday evening, it's a bit embarrassing when people have to be paid to watch your team; meeting Ray Stubbs in the car park one Saturday; and the moronic Mansfield fan who scaled the floodlight forcing a match to be abandoned when we were closing in on the play-offs.

"I remember my first Tranmere game," Katie began. "I'd broken my wrist and was in hospital; these horrid, stupid girls I went to school with had pushed me over and I broke my wrist!"

"That's cruel!" I said. I've never liked bullies; they're up there with tennis, glory hunters and That Bloody Stretford Mob.

"I know, it really hurt and the painkillers they gave me were hopeless!" Katie agreed. "I was unhappy in hospital until the Tranmere players paid a visit, the great Johnny King was with them," she added.

"What a man!" I said enthusiastically, realising straight away we had mutual admiration for the great man himself.

"A very nice man," Katie went on. "He told me that we'd be playing Aston Villa in the League Cup semi in a couple of days, my dad and brothers were going so I convinced them to take me along so I could cheer on the players who'd cheered me up! And we beat them 3-1!"

"I couldn't get to that game, I was sick; I had to listen to that game on the radio," I added.

"After that I was hooked; I come when I can now – I'll forego shopping for clothes and shoes so I can see Tranmere!" she stated. "Mind you, I would sooner see Tranmere than waltz around shopping all afternoon like a brain-dead bimbo!"

"I used to scrub dishes in a Chinese restaurant to supplement my Tranmere allowance!" I told her.

"I used to be a waitress in this grotty little restaurant; I was at college and needed to supplement my income!" Katie told me.

"Where was that?" I asked.

"It was called Bunty's, looked nice from the outside but was a complete dump inside!" she told me.

"I'm not familiar with it," I said.

"It was in Port Sunlight, my hometown," Katie advised.

"Oh, I occasionally get down there," I told her. "For work mainly!"

"Where do you live?" she asked.

"Rock Ferry," I informed her, proudly. "I was born there and grew up there – it still baffles me as a place but I wouldn't give it up for anything!"

She laughed and smiled her beautiful smile, her eyes glimmering beautifully. I looked at her and smiled, there was something I really needed to ask her. "Do you have a boyfriend?"

"Yes," she replied.

I felt my heart sink.

"His name is Jordan," she continued.

"How long have you seeing each other?" I asked.

"Just over a year," she informed me.

I felt a bit down but something told me this was right, something in her voice told me this was right. Something told me not to give up and something told me this girl was simply amazing and I was destined to spend my life with her. I had known her only a few hours but I was sure she was The One.

"What about you, Tommy? Do you have someone?" Katie asked with an optimistic smile.

"I've been single about a year now," I told her. "My last girlfriend didn't like playing second fiddle to the Super Whites!"

Katie smiled and bit her lip as if this was music to her ears. "She was a fool there," Katie replied. "The Rovers are a big part of my life!"

I laughed. "I decided if I ever let myself fall in love again it would have to be with a fellow Tranmere fan!" I explained.

"I better watch myself then!" said Katie, with a cheeky smile and a sexy flutter about her beautiful eyes.

Katie smiled then I smiled and when we looked at each other I thought I might have leant across the table where we were sat at and kissed her; suddenly I realised where we were and she was spoken for. There was an awkward silence for a few minutes between us.

"Can I be a gentleman and walk you home?" I offered before the awkwardness became too much.

"Certainly," she replied.

"Would you like another drink first?" I asked.

"Why not?" she replied rhetorically.

Katie started to tell me about Jordan; I didn't ask she just told me. He was unemployed and living off benefits; apparently it wasn't his fault because he had been to prison a few times and no one would employ him because of his criminal record. Apparently he had underachieved at school and was expelled for assaulting another pupil. Katie told me that he had turned over a new leaf after his last court appearance just before they had met and was seeking employment, and that he had only been arrested twice since they had started to date. His usual average arrest rate was about ten per annum. Assault, drink driving, drunk and disorderly, drunk and incapable, burglary, theft, joyriding, threatening behaviour, benefit fraud, hooliganism, he had done it all. The most disturbing crime in his record collection, I must say, was domestic abuse. I hate men who beat up women and I hate the ones who try to justify doing it even more. Katie tried to tell me he was provoked by his ex-girlfriend and he had had to hit her to defend himself. To me this guy sounded like he was scum of the earth; why do all the nice girls date assholes?

A few months earlier I'd met a very nice girl. I was in a club and I bumped into Sid; he had some friends with him from a bar he liked to frequent due to his lifestyle. He introduced me to the manager of the bar who had his sister with him. Straight away I was attracted to this guy's sister, her beautiful brown eyes and a friendly smile; she had an amazing figure and legs that went on forever. I chatted to her all night and genuinely thought there might be something between us. She was engaged, though. And she was engaged to an absolute 24-carat rotter. He shouted at her, he ran her confidence down, he verbally abused, and he struck her. She continually stuck up for him though even though she shouldn't have. I did try to get to know her but her vile fiancée would kick up a stink and become increasingly violent and aggressive; he had a God-given ability to turn up and cause trouble at any given time, at any given opportunity and at any given location, in particularly when he had not been invited or told where anyone was. I gave up when he threatened to slit my throat; I dropped him to the deck and decided to walk away.

The more Katie told me about Jordan the more I grew to hate him. It was incredible, I had never met him or been formally introduced to him but I hated him already. Katie told me she cooked his meals, she washed his clothes, she bought his drinks; he lived in a council flat and she rented her flat. She would regularly help pay his rent; what a freeloading jerk. The more she told me the more I could tell she didn't love this man, it sounded as if she felt she could do better. But if anything she sounded somewhat scared of him, as if she was some kind of slave in his grasp.

Katie told me something about her darling scumbag that triggered a deep emotion in me. Katie said she was horrified when he had told her about it. A few years earlier Jordan had been at a nightclub in Clifton Park when a bloke began to threaten him. Scared, Jordan had bottled this man. Jordan was arrested but the man didn't press charges, eight months later he got a kicking from his victim. The man inflicted broken ribs and a punctured lung on Jordan. Katie was shocked by what the man had done to Jordan. I said he had brought it on himself but Katie said it couldn't be justified, Jordan was human after all; Katie felt that it was possibly the psychological damage Jordan had suffered from the assault that had turned him into the person he was and he was simply a victim of circumstance, I guess she was trying to justify him and his actions. I didn't tell her but it couldn't have happened to a better person as far as I was concerned! One other thing I didn't say to Katie was I had a feeling that I might already know Jordan...

We got to her flat, the building was very nice, and it was clean and well kept. It wasn't plastered in graffiti or with horrid little kids knocking around bugging you for cash, drink and cigarettes then f-ing and blinding at you when you say no. There's nothing worse than horrid little shits whose schools can't discipline and parents won't discipline. If I had acted like that at their age I would never got away with it, my dad would have found out and

I would have been for the high jump. We got to her front door, "Does Jordan come to Rovers games with you?" I asked as Katie put her key in the lock.

"No, he claims he's a Chelsea fan!" she informed me as she opened the door. "So you could say he doesn't like football!"

She laughed. I found myself transfixed on her mouth then her eyes; her smile turned to a slightly more serious look. She hugged me, I put my hands around her waist, and we stood looking at each other with the kind of 'Should we? Shouldn't we?' look; slowly I found myself drawing my face closer to hers; I felt internal conflict, the brain said no but the heart said yes. I rested my forehead gently against hers, expecting a kiss to be on the cards. Katie turned away as she sensed the tension between us; she kissed me on the cheek. "I'll be seeing you then," she said.

"How about we go to the next home game?" I asked hopefully.

"I'm not sure," she answered, "money's a bit tight."

"I can pay for you..." I said with an air of optimism in my voice.

"I hardly know you, a few drinks is one thing but a home ticket is another!" she replied in a soft voice. "I could never let you do that! You're a really nice guy though..."

"Well if you do go to the game you know where I sit, come and find me," I advised. "I really like you, Katie..."

"I like you, too, Tommy..." she said.

We looked each other in the eyes; that thought of 'Should we? Shouldn't we?' ran through our minds again. "I'd better go," I finally said. "It's Southend we are playing next home game..." I added, hopefully.

"Okay..." she said softly. "I'll see if I can make it..." she added.

As I walked down the road, I looked back; she smiled and waved. I had a warm feeling inside me because I had met the most amazing girl in the world and I thought I might be in love!

I felt conflict though, she was taken. And she was taken by a complete and utter rotten scumbag. As I lit up a cigarette and walked off down the road something bugged me; it nagged at me, something I could not understand – why was she telling me everything about this revolting individual? She hardly knew me and she was telling me all about this stain on the underwear of life! Plus she introduced herself to me, she told me I was a nice, she said I was a loss to my ex and she should watch herself in case I fell in love with her.

Rock Ferry was surprisingly quiet that evening; as I walked down Bedford Avenue towards the station I saw someone I instantly recognised, an individual who you will learn was from one of the darkest moments of my past.

"How did the Rovers get on today?" he asked in a thick, and possibly fake, Scouse accent.

"We beat York 3-0," I told him.

He grunted. "Mickey Mouse rubbish! I just watched a proper team on TV – we put Southampton out at home! My bird and me watched it down the pub! Well, she's not my actual bird; she's just my shag on the side!" He smirked unpleasantly. "My stupid bitch of a girlfriend was up your dump!"

"Who's your team then?" I asked, my suspicions aroused.

"I'm a Chelsea fan!" my acquaintance told me with an arrogant smirk.

I felt my blood begin to simmer. I scowled as I sensed a glory hunter and an absolute rotter in my midst. "Londoner are you?" I asked with venom.

"What's it to you?!" he replied aggressively.

"Bit odd a Chelsea fan with an accent like yours?" I asked, sarcastically.

"Well, it's a free country!" he barked back.

I began to walk on; I had had enough of him.

"Oi!" he shouted, his ugly face turning an awful violet red colour.

"What do you want?!" I asked as I turned around, half expecting a fight; one thing I've learnt is to never let your guard down with people like this; believe me, I learnt the hard way.

"Got a spare cig?!" he snarled.

I took my fag pack out of my pocket and took one out, "Here!" I said passing one to him; almost instinctively I knew what he was going to ask. I looked in the packet at the few which were left then threw it at his head, "You'd better have some spare for later!"

CHAPTER TWO

The One; An Explanation

I've always been a great believer in 'The One'. By that I mean that there is a great One True Love for everybody; out there on this planet of sixty billion or so people there is somebody for everyone. However, back then in my thirty-one years on this planet I hadn't met said person out the sixty billion or so people designated for me; there had been a few times when I had believed that Miss Right aka The One had walked into my life but, unfortunately, either very quickly or very slowly that thought would be crushed like a polystyrene cup that Sid had spilt on the deck in the Johnny King Stand on any given Saturday at Prenton Park.

People would walk up to me and ask, "I'm surprised you're not married with a couple of kids, Tommy!" I would smile nervously then mutter something about how it just hadn't happened for me or it not being my thing; part of me had just come to accept that love, marriage and The One were never going to happen to me. A bit like Tranmere Rovers winning the European Cup. It was a potentially nice thought but in reality a non-starter.

There was many a time I led myself to believe that love was one of those things made up to make money, a nicely spun myth that people fall in love with other people who they worship like a god or goddess, spend copious amount of money on the other to the benefit of the local and national economies before they decided what the flip (or words to those effects) let's get married and have a big day of it, spending even more money. Would that ever happen to me? A lot of the time I doubted it. I wondered – many a time, I would lie in bed of an evening pondering whether this was 'it' and that I would live my life in lonely misery. Then I remembered that pledge to myself when I was six that I would never get married because I would be far too embarrassed to kiss a girl in front of my family. I guessed of the sixty billion or so people there were on the planet that there wasn't one for me. I must be the exception to the rule of The One. Love was just one of those things that happened to other people.

When I looked at The One, the One for me was ultimately the Rovers. Let's face it, I spent copious amounts of money on following the Rovers and I had dedicated the best part of the past three decades to the Rovers, I had followed them through thick and thin, mostly thin but both thick and thin. Were the Super Whites my true other half? I did view Prenton Park like a temple and worshipped the ground a certain Mr King walked on!

Over the years the Rovers had cost me many relationships, from the odd broken date to women walking out on me. All the women I seemed to date never had time for the Rovers; even the ones who said they liked football never had time for the Rovers. I told myself that should I be prepared to allow another woman into my life she must be Super White Army through and through. And by that I mean a Tranmere Rovers fan and not a member of the Nazi League!

As I lay there in bed the Sunday evening after I met Katie I began to think, I had only just met her but Katie ticked all my boxes: she was beautiful, an amazing person, intelligent, she had beautiful eyes, captivating eyes and, most importantly, she was a Tranmere Rovers fan. As a girlfriend she would be ideal, tolerant and supportive of all things Super and White, happier in the stands at Prenton than traipsing around Liverpool looking for bargains at the shops, a girl who is happy to talk about 'that disgraceful performance last night' and not bitch about other women's fashion senses and who's shagging who. But then again men are bigger bitches than women will ever be; have you ever heard us talk about football? Claws out or what!

Laying there I couldn't help but think of the future and

mainly a fortnight on Saturday when the Super Whites would take on Southend United on the hallowed turf of Prenton Park; I hoped Katie would be there, could she possibly be The One? I knew I had to see her again

The next home game came and went. We beat Southend United with a goal from Marlon Broomes. Katie wasn't there; first I felt hollow and then deflated. Sid chuntered away through the whole game; nothing he said sank in. Apart from Broomes' deflected first-half strike and Sid performing his party trick, the game was dead. A Southend player threw himself on the deck in typical over-the-top fashion pretending to be hurt trying to win a penalty kick, the ref caught him as even Stevie Wonder could have seen that the Tranmere player had got the ball. The crowd in the Kop End spent the rest of the game barracking him. Good for them.

I've always believed, and you might agree with this, that any footballers who act like prima donnas and throw temper tantrums deserved the abuse they get. Are they not supposed to be men? Nothing is more cringe-inducing than watching a grown man throw himself on the deck, rolling around pretending to be hurt, trying to gain an advantage through blatant cheating; the worst part is the managers and so-called fans who try to imply that this 'part of the modern game'; then again they're usually the first to start wailing if it happens against their team.

After the match I had a couple of rare bad pints in the Prenton Park, I walked home full of a feeling of deflation and I must have lost around two packs of cigarettes to Rock Ferry Tobacco Duty. The feeling of deflation is horrid. I've had that feeling many times; knock-backs from girls; failed exams; realising you're not as good at something as you thought you were; supporting Tranmere Rovers.

But this deflation felt different. I couldn't put my finger on it. When Rovers were beaten in the 2000 League Cup final this didn't feel as bad, nor did it feel this bad when Rovers got relegated in 2001; that FA Cup Quarter final loss to Liverpool the same season where I blew two hundred quid at the bookies didn't make me feel this bad; even when a certain Mr King was relieved of his duties as manager and moved up to the boardroom it didn't feel this bad. It was a different kind of deflation. I suppose I now knew how the Three Musketeers felt.

The Three Musketeers were a trio of gents who went in the Prenton Park pub all week long and had played the football pools religiously for as long as I could remember. One fateful Saturday in May 1999 they were on for a big win. There was one game outstanding on the fixture sheet and with Carlisle United, rock bottom of the football league, trailing to Plymouth Argyle 1-0, it was still on and Carlisle faced the next season in the non-leagues, well, that was till well into injury time when a man named Jimmy Glass, in desperation, went up the Plymouth penalty area for a late corner. With the last kick of the game Carlisle United goalkeeper Jimmy Glass scored a goal for his team that kept Carlisle in the football league and at the same time blowing the Three Musketeers' winnings. For the Three Musketeers the words Carlisle and Jimmy Glass are still sore to this day. I guess I understood what it was like to have something special suddenly snatched away.

I tried to keep my spirits up – you know keep telling myself that there are plenty more fish in the sea and that I hardly knew her so she couldn't be that special. By the time I turned the key in my front door I had convinced myself I would be okay. I sat down in front of the TV with a tuna baguette or two and told myself maybe I should go out and try and find a nice young woman like the girl with the nice hair who works in the cafe on Church Road. After deciding an early night would be best for me, I had set my heart on asking the nice Polish lady who lives down the road from Sid out on a date and that would be it. By the time I decided to bag up my jars of change it was 3 a.m. and I couldn't sleep because I was thinking of Katie. I also concluded that she must be special otherwise she wouldn't make me feel like I did.

Usually in a situation like this a cold wet nose and a set of bushy whiskers is a great help. Dolly is my cat, a saggy grey and white who my family adopted from a rescue shelter; she had belonged to an old lady who had passed away and was taken to the shelter. Very quickly Dolly decided that she didn't belong to me, I belonged to her. Many times when I'd be sick or unhappy she knew when a gentle head butt, a cold wet nose and a soft purring was appropriate. When I decided to leave home Dolly got distressed and after an interesting visit to a pet psychiatrist (yes these people do exist!) it was decided she was best off living with me so in she moved. On this very rare occasion Dolly's affection didn't work. Dejected, she curled up, sulkily, and went to sleep as I bagged up the change.

Ninety pounds in twenty pees, forty-five pounds in ten pences, 70 quid in five pences and nine pound in copper was the grand total which when combined added up to £214. I also found the usual assortment of Euros, foreign change and outdated silver and copper. It never surprises me as to how I can accumulate so much change; I've always managed to accumulate it, I never pass the exact change and I'll deliberately buy things that have a 5p as the last decimal just to get five pees. The only loose change I ever carry are £2, £1 and 50 pences. Once bagged up I would take it down to the bank and it would contribute towards my life savings. It's important to save, believe me; you never know what fate will do to you. One minute you can be rolling in gold, the next you can't see where you are going for all the dust. I hope that makes sense...

I'm self-employed which means I have to work to make my money and if I do take time off it can be costly. Sometimes getting to the bank can be a bit awkward but it's an absolute essential; if I didn't go to the bank to deposit my money I wouldn't be able to pay the bills and if I didn't pay the bills I would have my utilities switched off. There was a game against Leyton Orient slowly drawing near and I was pondering whether I should go to the game as I waited in the queue: was it really worth it supporting Tranmere anymore; should I say stuff this and sell my soul to a multinational Corporation in the Premiership? Then somebody spoke and I felt into a dream. I started thinking of Blackburn, Lancashire and its four thousand holes; they now knew how many holes it took to fill the Albert Hall but how many holes would it take, I wondered, to fill Prenton Park? Oh boy...

I've never been keen on queues. There is always someone who takes forever and then there'll be someone who doesn't know why they are there; plus it's almost a given that someone will stop to have a casual conversation with the cashier or shop assistant about what they did or are going to do at the weekend and please don't get me started on push ins! The types of people who simply can't wait their turn then take offence when people tell them to wait. I had the misfortune to meet one of these people in a nightclub I've long since stopped going into once I realised it was a dump. For some reason I went to this dump one night and whilst waiting an age for a libation this individual began wiping his nose on my jacket in what I believe was a nauseating attempt to jump the queue. And when I politely told him to get lost or words to that effect, he took exception and kicked off; and when I got served in front of him he accused me of pushing in. Some people!

I filled in a paying-in slip and stood for what felt like an eternity in the queue clutching a bag with the change bags in, as the person ahead of me began a conversation with the cashier about how the weekend went. When I finally reached the head of the queue, I dumped my change on the counter. "I'd like to pay this change in!" I muttered with my head down.

"Off to the game on Saturday, Tommy?" asked a familiar voice.

I looked up and was greeted by a beautiful smile, "I'll be

there," I beamed. "Wind, rain or shine, Katie! I'm Super White Army through and through!"

I called around for Katie at 2 p.m. that Saturday, we walked to the ground and had two pints before kick-off. Chris Shuker bagged a goal either side of the break and although Orient added a consolation goal, we walked away 2-1 winners.

On the way up to the ground that afternoon I had a little chat with Katie, nothing serious about The One or marriage, just a nice cosy little chat, important but cosy.

"So how long have you worked at the bank?" I recall asking her.

"About four years," she told me. "It's okay, the pay's decent and so are the benefits!"

"What about the people you work with?" I asked.

"They can be annoying and irritating at times but they're okay!" Katie said to me. "What about you, what do you do?" she asked.

"I'm a plumber," I advised her. "I work for myself!" I added.

"How long have you done that?" Katie enquired.

"About six years," I replied.

"How old are you?" Katie asked.

"I'm thirty-one," I told her, "how about you, Katie, how old are you? If that isn't too much of a rude question to ask!" I added.

Katie smiled, "I'm twenty-nine!" she answered. "When's your birthday?" she asked.

"15th of April," I replied.

Katie suddenly stopped open-mouthed and shocked, "It isn't, is it?" she said.

"It is," I told her and I took my wallet out of my pocket and removed my driving license to show her. "Same day as Johnny King!"

"That's the same day as me, too!" Katie added as she took her license out of her bag to show me.

From then on Katie was my best friend. Every home game she would be there with me; when we weren't at Prenton we would text, e-mail and phone each other regarding all things Tranmere. The more time we spent together the more I denied I was in love with her. I wanted to get closer to her but I couldn't; I remember when I made the mistake a few years prior of getting close to a girl I loved very deeply knowing she was out of bounds, she was only nineteen but I cared for her very deeply in a short space of time and I think I fell in love; letting myself get too close to her was a mistake, the pain of being so close but at the same time so far away was just too much for me to bear. I couldn't let myself go through that with Katie. Falling in love with her was not an option; well it was not an option if she was taken that is.

I hardly knew anything about her except her name was Katie, she worked in a bank, her boyfriend was a complete tosser and she supported Tranmere Rovers. Following a win against Norwich when Bas Savage scored with a spectacular overhead volley, I decided I must slowly get to know her as a person. Over the next few games we slowly got to know each other, we both happily agreed our friendship was simply platonic, although we would both confess it wasn't later. The most important thing I found out about Katie was the man who drew us both to Tranmere: Johnny King.

We would sit and talk about the Johnny King Era all night; it was our great age. Yes, John Aldridge led us to a League Cup Final and sent us on a two-year giant-killing spree, but to us Johnny King was the man. Over and over we would recall our favourite Rovers moments under Johnny King, beating Aston Villa, the three successive play-offs, the LDV Vans trophy win in 1990 thanks to Jim Steele's header, the giant killing and promotion in 88-89. Those are the moments when you support a small club that make it all worthwhile. Little did we realise that we were to have one of those special moments ourselves.

Ever since that two-season spell in the early part of the century when we reached back-to-back Cup quarter finals, the FA Cup has always had a place in my heart. It was the fifth round and we had dispatched a few minnows over the first three rounds – Eastbourne Borough, Swindon Town and York City; in the fourth round we had our fellow League One team Exeter City, so I guess we were overdue a big one. And they don't come much bigger than our Merseyside neighbours Liverpool, multiple winners of the Cup, the league and European Cup (I always call it by its correct name and not the Champions League!).

It was a 2 o'clock kick-off on a Sunday afternoon, Katie came round to my house at 10 a.m. that Sunday morning, we enjoyed some roast beef and Yorkshire pudding with a selection of vegetables – Dolly sat on a chair by the table with a look as if to say, 'what a loving, friendly cat I am and have I ever told you how much I love you and would you like to share your food with me?' look. Katie and I talked about the 1-0 defeat to Charlton Athletic in midweek thanks to a shocking decision by the ref, Man United getting dumped out of the Cup the day before by Stoke City, then commented on Jimmy Hill's chin and its other possible uses in a highly mature moment. Dolly took an instant liking to Katie and Katie took an instant liking to Dolly; she spent the morning under our feet and showed great interest in the roast beef. A good relationship between cat and potential girlfriend was another good omen!

Sid wouldn't be joining us that home game; he had to go to Scotland to attend his niece's wedding where he would be updating his family on the case of him with the limp who lives at 33 and her who does Tuesdays and Thursdays at the post office amongst other monumental gossip. There were times that Sid was just like an old woman, he was the gossip king and the leader of the local net-curtain twitchers; if anything gossip-wise happened Sid would be one of the first to know. We walked up to the ground at 1.20 p.m. On the way Katie explained Jordan had got drunk and was arrested the night before; Jordan had used his one phone call to phone her up to blame her for him getting arrested. It wasn't his fault apparently; someone had been giving him dirty looks so he HAD to kick their head in. What an arse, I thought! Katie tried to play the dutiful girlfriend but I could tell from her voice she was ashamed, embarrassed and intimidated by him; there's nothing worse than a lovely girl trying to justify the actions of a complete bastard or just as bad any girl who will follow any complete swine blindly as if their beloved is some kind of god despite the fact they treat their lady like dirt. She went on to add that she would really like me to meet Jordan, we would be great friends by her reckoning, and she said rather painfully that he was a nice guy. Was he hell! Why do nice girls like tossers?!

My first real girlfriend was a Welsh girl named Lynda. Before me she dated a string of rotters – pimps, fraudsters, druggies, drug dealers, a paedophile and even a murderer, they were all vile and false people who wanted to use her for some sex. They were people who exploited her vulnerability, they were people who didn't care about her; only themselves. People who said that they knew her slated her, they called her a slag, a tart; made out she was a drug addict, some called her a prostitute – they called her everything they could. They didn't know her, only I did; only I saw her for who she truly was. I saw Lynda as a kind person, a loving person, someone who wanted to be loved; someone who hadn't had a good start in life, someone who deserved a chance. Lynda was a just the product of a bad environment.

She was a product of a broken home, her father had walked out on her alcoholic mother when she was four, by the time she was eight she was in care and was adopted. Constantly at logger-heads with her adoptive parents she rebelled and fell in with the wrong crowd. She lost her virginity young, squandered a singing and acting talent; Lynda became hooked on Valium and fell pregnant to a vile drug dealer. She would later miscarry when he punched her in the stomach. She went with plenty of men and a few women who she thought would be able to give her what she felt she needed. When I got together with her I saw the real her, a person who needed to be loved. I tried to give her what she truly needed and not some cheap thrill or meaningless sexual encounter. I wanted to give her the security, safety, affection and love I felt she truly deserved.

I tried to give her all that. It failed. I became paranoid, she still hung around with the wrong crowd, we drank too much, and I listened to the wrong people, so did she. After nine turbulent months our relationship imploded following a stupid row in a nightclub; a womanising idiot hit on her and I warned her off. She I felt I was too protective, we argued, she cheated, we cried, we split. We patched things up and remained friends; she went back to her old ways of dating rotters and taking drugs. A few months later she fell pregnant, the father was unknown. She was swept off her feet by a complete swine who promised her the world. They moved to Liverpool and he dumped her a few months later before he resurfaced in Rock Ferry and became a member of local government. I've heard she now lives in Birmingham, her daughter was taken into care and she works as a stripper; a few people have told me they thought I had had a lucky escape on that one, sometimes I think I could've given her a better life. Never mind, eh?

When a so-called big team plays its small, overlooked local rival you can always guarantee a game. The small team always wants to silence the loudmouths who will be ready to boast to all and sundry at the next given opportunity. Some glory hunters posing as Liverpool fans had told us on our way to the match having collected our Rock Ferry Tobacco Duty that Tranmere had no right to be there in the Cup in the first place, that the match was in the bag, Tranmere were going to be stuffed like a Christmas turkey and they were off to the pub up the road to watch the match because the prices at Prenton Park football ground were too high and that the Prenton Park pub was always full of white-nosers except during the game but it was crap in there anyway. When I asked them about the current cost of admission to Anfield they were unable to give me an accurate answer, considering they hadn't been for a while; well, considering they hadn't been at all in their lives. The usual expert drivel from glory-hunting armchair experts. They must have felt daft as they nursed their pints in the pub during the game.

It was an end-to-end game which is the type of game I like to watch, plenty of action and plenty of incidents, Joe Collister made a fine string of saves, Liverpool hit the woodwork, Tranmere hit it once as well, then forced the 'pool to clear off their line. My heart jangled all game, so did Katie's. Midway through the second half just after a Chris Shuker shot had flashed past the far post, I felt her hand run down my arm, Katie looked across at me and then her soft cold hand slipped into mine. It stayed there. With fifteen minutes left, Marlon Broomes was brought down a couple of yards from the 18-yard box. The referee awarded a free kick to Tranmere. Alan Mahon lined up the free kick; he took a few steps in before slapping it into the top right corner of the goal. Prenton Park erupted like we had won the Cup itself. I turned to Katie and we hugged, we smiled at each other. Then I kissed her.

We stood there transfixed on each other for what felt like an eternity with a look of disbelief on our faces. It had happened, it had finally happened; I shouldn't have kissed Katie but it felt so right though. Suddenly, I had that feeling once more like everything around us was going ahead in slow motion; the fans jumping up and down, the applause, the cheers. I looked into her beautiful eyes, everything around us seemed to slow down; I stroked a couple of stray hairs away from her beautiful eyes, I gently placed my hand on her smooth cheek and kissed her again. She accepted. I must say I've kissed a fair few girls and Katie was easily the best. There was perfect lip contact, soft lips, perfect tongue and a hint of a smile. The final ten minutes of the match were irrelevant. I wrapped my arm around Katie as she rested her head against me. I had finally found The One. Suddenly a Paul McLaren long-range shot rocketed into the back of the net, the crowd erupted once more. The Reds were in shock and the Rovers had made the quarter finals. We hugged and kissed, "I love you, Katie!" I whispered in Katie's ear.

"That's okay," she whispered back with a smile. "I love you, too!"

CHAPTER THREE

Love and Other Complicated Matters

A lot of man hours were to be lost the following morning on the Wirral Peninsula when many a Wirralite failed to make it to work. The whole of Birkenhead was abuzz for the rest of Sunday and most of the next week following the news of the Cup upset. For the sporting media Birkenhead was a hotspot and Tranmere Rovers were the hottest topical subject. Local people would be stopped in the street by the major broadcasters and newspapers then interviewed; they would say how brilliant it was for the town and club plus how they never missed a home game and they had supported the Rovers through thick and thin for so and so many years. Pity I didn't recognise any of them. I would have been able to tell them I saw them on the TV next time I saw them at Prenton Park, well just in case they just happened to know where that was. In the style of the shopkeeper from *Mr Benn* 'lifelong' Tranmere fans appeared suddenly as if from nowhere.

There's a fair few types of so-called fans who get on my nerves. Fair-weather fans, the type who support a team when it is convenient are one, they pledge their allegiance to another team or even claim they aren't interested in football but should their small local team do well they crawl out of the woodwork en mass to 'support THEIR team'. I recall a non-league team drawing one of the Premiership big guns in the Cup one year; suddenly with a trip away to a major team the non-league team had a following support of 5,000 people more than 3 times its average gate for home games.

I've spoke of glory hunters and they never cease to shock me. One minute the alleged fans would be screaming at a player simply because they do not play for their team, then they will be singing their praises when said player is linked in a move to their team before slating them when they reject that move and eventually supporting them when the player switches to another team along with the glory hunter, just like that glory hunter I went to school with and the obsession he had with Alan Shearer. He insisted Shearer was hopeless, well, crap was the word he used but Shearer was his first pick for a fantasy football team; the glory hunter insisted he was a better player than Shearer despite not even playing for the school team or a local junior team; and then he couldn't believe that Alan Shearer would want to play for another team than Man United if he left Blackburn Rovers; he joined Newcastle United. I hope that all makes sense because it doesn't to me!

Armchair experts do my head in; they always know who should be picked and who should be dropped, they write into the letters pages you find on Teletext to vent their bloated opinions, they know everything about everything, an expert on every sport and every sporting issue. The ones who think they know about cricket amaze me; they know who should be picked and who should be dropped, who is a good player, they bleat on about player X until you're sick to death of hearing about them. They write off young player X before they've had a chance and believe they are right on every subject they choose to flap their gums about. I must say though that 99% of the time the armchair expert gets it wrong.

Much as I slate the fair-weather fans, the glory hunters and armchair experts, they aren't the worst people associated with football. Not even That Bloody Stretford Mob are the worst; they have a lot of dedicated fans and I know a few United fans that are actually alright. Oh no, the old glory hunters et al don't even come close; we all know who the scourge of the football world are: that is the hooligans. People who use a game as an excuse for a fight, people who make other people's lives miserable and ruin their enjoyment of one of life's simple pleasures, pathetic individuals who ruin other people's livelihoods for nothing more than a game, the morons who drive away real fans willing to pay good money for a bit of enjoyment. I feel sorry for anyone who gets caught up in the violence caused by these pathetic morons; families, pensioners, genuine fans all terrified of the crucible of hatred stirred up by those rotten fools hell-bent on causing trouble. They might have watched a good match, they might have watched a poor match but they don't need their day ruined by these wretched fools. Of anyone associated with football it's the hooligans I really hate. In fact, there was a time I met a former football hooligan.

I was down in London with an ex of mine to see her family, officially for a visit and, unofficially to be vetted for my suitability for potential matrimonial purposes. I guess I failed that purpose as I got a talk shortly after my return to Birkenhead explaining that things had 'run their course', it would be better if we were just friends and that was that. What a load of cobblers. I digress. In London I had slipped out one evening to a nearby pub for a quiet drink, and a man in the pub noticed my Rovers scarf.

"Football fan are you?" he had asked. "I'm a Southampton man myself; nothing like the match and a punch-up on a Saturday!" he added with a foolish smirk, the type of smirk that says I don't know why I'm smirking.

Normally I would have walked away from this man but this time for a change I sat and decided to listen to this individual; the man proceeded to tell me how he got into hooliganism in the early eighties; unemployed, nothing to do, he began to hang around with a group of ne'er-do-wells who enjoyed nothing more than meeting up for a punch-up with the rival supporters before and/or after the match. He told me of the buzz of excitement he got from the conflict, the feeling of empowerment he felt as he beat another hooligan senseless, the respect of his firm when they came out on top and the feeling of status he felt when people identified him as a hooligan, how the younger thugs would look up to him. There was an almost eerie romance about the tales he told me.

But my acquaintance told me things changed; he found employment and a girlfriend, his priorities changed quickly when she became pregnant. He stopped going along on Saturdays and things look set to change for the better until he was coerced into going along one Saturday, 'for old time's sake'. He got eighteen months. When he got out his child was born, and seven months later when he was sent down again for another eighteen months his girlfriend left with his child, who he had never seen since. "He's about your age now!" my acquaintance advised me.

The man told me that for about a decade he was in the repeat cycle of prison and hooliganism; a few months out then a year or two in; it was as if he didn't know any better. He told me that one fateful Sunday afternoon in the early nineties things finally changed. During the midst of a mass brawl an innocent bystander was dragged into the brawl then violently and brutally kicked to death by others in the mob. His crime was simply being stood in the wrong place at the wrong time and wearing the wrong colours. The former hooligan said he pleaded guilty to the offences he was later charged with; although he was not directly responsible for the man's death he felt tremendous remorse and guilt. He vowed to go straight and when he had served his stint he was determined to never go back inside.

After being released from what would be his final stint, he straightened out his act. He became a youth worker and dedicated his life to stopping others from falling into the cycle he had found himself in many years before. "I don't go to the game anymore," he told me when I asked if he still went to Southampton games, "it brings back too many bad memories."

Following the match I went to the Prenton Park where I had a few games of pool with Katie and then we sat down and talked; we talked properly. Not about football, not about Jimmy Hill's chin, not even about Johnny King; we talked. We got deeper than we had before, not the basic application form details we already knew about each other; this time when talked we finally got to really know each other, our loves, our loathes, the people and things we love and essentially what made us the people we are. That quarter final against Liverpool and especially that kiss really changed everything.

About 10 o'clock I walked her home, though on the way we both enjoyed a cod and chips from the nearby chippy. We got to her flat and after enjoying another long lingering kiss I asked her out.

"No," she said with a sad smile as we stood holding each other. "I'm still with Jordan."

"You're too good for him," I told her sadly, "you're an amazing person and you deserve a much better person than him!"

"But he's my boyfriend," she added, I noted the look of disappointment in her eyes. "I have to be faithful to him, he would to me..."

"I love you, Katie!" I declared, my lips lingering close to hers once more. "In the words of the Ramones, I want to be your boyfriend!"

"And I love you, Tommy!" she admitted. "But I'm seeing Jordan. I can't cheat on him, he would never forgive me!"

I trudged down towards the Rock Ferry station, there was something I didn't like about how Katie said she couldn't cheat and how Jordan would never forgive her. It wasn't that she had said she could never cheat, it was the way she had said it; there was the sound in her voice of fear when she said Jordan would never forgive her and if she did he would really hurt her. I got a horrible feeling deep down. Suddenly I feared for Katie's well-being; suddenly I knew I was in love, I knew I was in love with Katie because I cared about her and I cared a lot about her.

"Oi!" said a voice as I passed the bookmakers at the bottom of

Bedford Avenue. I turned to my left. "Got a spare fag?" said the individual.

"No," I lied, "I'm all out!"

"Oh," grunted my acquaintance. "How did Tranmere do?" he asked noticing my team colours

"Beat Liverpool 2-0," I informed him.

"Didn't see it myself; too busy shagging some bird!" he announced, not at all interested in the upset result I had told him but quite happy to brag about his sexual exploits. "I only got out of the cells this afternoon!" he added with an arrogant sneer on his face.

"Good for you!" I replied, insincerely.

"Better not let my bird find out though!" he sneered. "Where do I know you from?" he asked aggressively after a pause, the tempo in his voice clearly changing .

"About two months ago you bummed some smokes from me," I advised. "Support Chelsea don't you?"

"Yeah!" my acquaintance grunted. "Beat Preston yesterday!"

"I better get going," I said, not wishing to speak to this loser any longer.

My acquaintance glared at me, "Where do I know you from?" he asked menacingly.

"No idea!" I replied with a laugh and walked off not letting my guard down. It sometimes surprises me as to how easily some people forget.

Being a plumber by trade I have learnt over a short period of time that it is very important that I concentrate on my job. It's extremely difficult to unblock a U-bend when you're thinking about a girl you go to the weekend's football match with and how fine she looked in particular on Saturday night in that blue denim miniskirt. I also found that customers are not particularly sympathetic when you ruin their carpet or break something. It can be quite costly, too. I never like to overcharge and customers are definitely not sympathetic if you try to add an expense racked up as a result of you breaking something because you can't keep your mind on the job; plus they really wouldn't care if you think you're in love and definitely don't want to know how fine she does look in that certain blue denim miniskirt. I did find one sympathetic ear on that Tuesday afternoon though.

"Here you go, Tommy, dry yourself off," said Jean, my grandmother's best friend, as she passed me a towel. I dried my face and soaked up as much water from my drenched T-shirt as I could.

"I can't believe I forgot to turn off the stopcock, Jean!" I said, jokingly; though thoroughly disgusted with myself for making such a schoolboy error like a defender who has passed the ball across an open goalmouth and it's nearly ended up in the back of the net.

"What's wrong, love?" she asked, sensing that there was something praying on my mind. I'd known Jean for years. I had grown up with her practically as family. She was also my own personal agony aunt; at any time I knew I could turn to her for a sympathetic ear, a cup of tea and advice. All the key times in my life she'd been there when I needed her to be, the heartache, the agony and not just from the Rovers. School, love, family, she'd always be the one to see me through. Jean was even the person who recommended the pet psychiatrist when Dolly started having her moments.

After a mouthful of tea and half a bourbon cream I took a deep breath, "I've fallen in love…" I announced.

Jean smiled, "Pretty girl is she?"

"Gorgeous!" I replied.

"Where did you meet her?" asked Jean.

"At Prenton Park – in the Johnny King Stand," I informed Jean.

"That's nice! Like the football does she?" Jean enquired.

"Yes," I said, "She's been a fan since the '94 League Cup semis against Villa!"

"I haven't been since Harry died," Jean recalled with a sad smile. "It doesn't feel the same without him!"

"I do miss him," I remembered. Jean's late husband Harry had been close friends with my grandad. "There would be me, my dad, Uncle Billy, Grandad, Harry and Sid every home game – now's it's just me and Sid!"

"What about your lady friend?" asked Jean. "How often does she go to Prenton?"

"Oh, she's there as much as she can!" I said to Jean.

"What's her name?" asked Jean.

"Katie," I said, in an almost dreamlike state as I uttered her beautiful name. "She's two years younger than me, she works in a bank and is originally from Port Sunlight plus we share the same birthday, it's the same as Johnny King's!"

"She sounds nice – what do you like best about her?" Jean enquired.

"I like her company..." I said.

"That's a good start!" she told me. "So why are you attracted to her?"

I paused. "She has lovely eyes and a beautiful smile..." I sighed, dreamily.

"Did you ask her out?" Jean asked.

"Yes..." I replied, glumly.

"And what was the result?" Jean enquired.

"She said no..." I answered, sadly.

"Move on, Tommy, she's not interested," Jean advised.

"I think she does like me...we've kissed...at the Liverpool game last Sunday..." I explained

"Oh..." Jean said, with a slight realisation.

"I told her I loved her and she said she loved me!" I told Jean.

"So why won't she go out with you?" Jean asked, confused by my tale of woe.

"She has a boyfriend – he's a nasty piece of work..." I explained, sadly.

Jean pondered, "Just make sure you are friends. She'll grow closer to you and after spending time with you she'll end up realising she's better with you. I'm sure she'll pick you...especially after the way you kissed her!"

That night I lay in bed with my lovely Katie on my mind. Dolly had curled up next to me. As I stroked her and rubbed her behind the ear she purred, she has a very therapeutic purr. A cat's purr can be very soothing as can a cat's soft fur. A memory was suddenly jerked. I was thinking about a goal Blackpool had scored at the weekend; it had been a clumsy goal, a cross that had just somehow ended up in the back of net. A few years earlier I had been to Blackpool and just as a bit of a joke I went to see a fortune teller. She told me my fortune and specifically I would marry a girl called Kate or Katie. Had her prophecy come true? Only time would tell! But as I tried to sleep something Jean had said to me really bugged me, what it was I wasn't sure, but something definitely bugged me...

Over a week had passed since we beat Liverpool in the Cup; the media circus that had followed had now died down and Birkenhead would no longer be on the media's menu until the quarter finals so all the fair-weather fans had forgotten that there was even a football team in Birkenhead. We played an away game at Walsall midweek. I couldn't go as I had to be up for work the next day so I had a few in the pub with Sid as we waited for the results to come in. Well, actually I sat unhappily in the corner of the pub looking miserable whilst Sid hissed away.

"I see United got put out the European Cup," Sid announced, I didn't reply, "by Barcelona," I still didn't reply. "Matthew will be disappointed..."

"Who's Matthew?" I asked suddenly with an element of bemusement, half-awake to Sid's ramblings.

"You're back to life!" hissed Sid.

"Who's this Matthew you just mentioned?" I asked with aroused nosiness on the levels of a Manx cat.

"He's a friend of mine," Sid told me.

"He's your friend?" I questioned. "Is this a special friend of yours?"

"Yes," said Sid, "about your age, enjoys his sport..."

"Does he?" I asked, not really interested in what Sid was saying any longer.

"United fan – well, he used to support Chelsea...and Arsenal...plus Leeds...and even Blackburn for a while," Sid informed me. "Something of a Ryan Giggs fan!" he added. "And Nick Faldo... keeps banging on about him and how great he was..."

"That's nice," I replied, now completely disinterested.

"What is up with you?" asked Sid.

"There's nothing up, Sid!" I said, glumly.

"There is!" Sid snapped back. "There's something up with you; you've been a right misery! Like him from North Road with the gambling problem when he loses a packet in the bookmakers!"

"I'm tired, I've had a tough day...tough week actually and it's only Tuesday!" I tried to explain. "I had a run in with an exceptionally violent showerhead this morning..."

"How's your back, Tommy?" Sid asked, rudely.

"It's rather sore to be honest, Sid..." I told him, flatly.

Sid sighed, "You're lying!" he said to me, sharply.

"I am not!" I retorted. "My back is killing me!"

"Don't lie!" said Sid. "I know when you're lying, you always say you're tired and have a sore back – just like you did with that bird who has the face like a bag full of spanners that keeps trying it on with you!"

"Which one is that?" I asked, trying to place the young woman in question.

"That one you can't stand, she kept trying to talk to you and when you wouldn't she said 'you don't like me, do you' to which you said 'I'm just tired'!" Sid explained. "AND you had a sore back!"

"No, I can't place her..." I replied, hazily

Sid snapped his fingers, "Caroline!" he said. "Her name's Caroline; she has a face like a bag full of spanners!"

A horrid chill went down the back of my spine and I shuddered as I remembered the young woman in question. "Oh her!" I recalled with a quiver in my voice. "The Attention Seeking Mental Case!"

"I remember when she hijacked that karaoke!" added Sid. "She tried to tell that joke, it went on for 15 minutes, it had no punchline and she never finished it!"

"I remember when she got barred!" I said.

"What did she do?" asked Sid.

"She did the treble!" I informed him.

"What's that?!" asked Sid with a hint of trepidation.

"She was found in the bog one night on the floor; vomiting, pissing and shitting!" I explained.

"Charming!" said Sid, sarcastically. "Leon at Garland's told me of a girl who did that in there!" We both laughed. "So what is up with you?" he asked in slightly more serious tone.

"I told you – nothing!" I said firmly.

"It's that bird, isn't it?" probed Sid. I was silent. "That one with the big boobs!"

"Katie has nothing to do with it," I replied. "I'm just tired, my back is feeling a bit sore and I need a bit of a kip." I added, "Anyway I've not really noticed the size of her boobs!"

Sid gave me a condescending look, "You've always gone for girls with big boobs!" he snorted. "Don't tell me you haven't had a good look!"

"I haven't really looked..." I began.

"They call her Funbags, you know," Sid told me in a rude tone.

"Who calls who Funbags?" I asked, sharply.

"The regulars in here," Sid explained, "the regulars'

nickname for Katie in here is Funbags because her Bristols are so impressive! They say 'here comes that Tommy with that girl with the big knockers, you know, Funbags'!"

"As I said, Sid," I began, "I haven't really noticed them; there's other qualities Katie possesses, like her smile!"

"You like her smile?" Sid asked.

"Yes I do!" I told him.

"I knew you liked her lips!" Sid answered.

"How do you know that?" I asked Sid.

"That all makes sense now!" Sid laughed. "You haven't noticed her Bristols because you were too busy necking with her weren't you?"

"What do you mean?" I asked Sid cautiously.

"The other week when we beat Liverpool, you were necking with her!" Sid replied.

I was suddenly concerned; Sid hadn't been at the game, he was at his niece's wedding in Scotland. "Watched it on the box, didn't I?" he pointed out when I asked him how he knew about my kiss with Katie. Sid explained that the coverage cut to the stands and an audience of potentially all of England, Scotland, Wales, Northern Ireland, the Isle of Man and the Channel Islands plus people with satellite on the continent would have witnessed me kissing Katie.

There and then a horrible thought ran through my mind; it was Katie, she could be in trouble. She couldn't come to the game on Saturday; it wasn't a case that she was skint, which was Katie's usual excuse for not being able to attend a home game. She said she was sick. I didn't believe it, she wasn't the type who would let illness get in the way of the Rovers; maybe a lack of funds but certainly not illness. Suddenly what Jean had said had some substance; something told me there was a problem. I suddenly realised what had been bugging me so much for the past week.

I finished my drink, left the pub, then I walked to Katie's flat - well I downed my pint and sprinted to Katie's – Sid said he had never seen me move so fast except for the time I tried mild because it was going cheap. I would have made a joke along the lines of being beware of mild going cheap but I wasn't in a jovial mood. My suspicions were unfortunately confirmed; Katie was sporting an unstylish pair of dark glasses, her beautiful eyes had been blackened. She told me an unconvincing tale of how she had fallen over and banged her face. I knew that thug was responsible. I asked about him and she gave it away. The tone of her voice and her mannerisms were ones of fear when she just happened to mention that a certain thug had seen a particular football match on the television between a particular Birkenhead football team and their certain Merseyside neighbours.

Her darling boyfriend had dropped round the day after the game, they had argued and she had 'fallen' over; when I asked about how she fell, Katie said she had tripped over the coffee table when she walked away from Jordan as they argued, her explanation sounded forced and false. I knew he had hit her, my blood began to boil. Seeing her beautiful eye blemished made me feel so angry, I calmly left her flat after wishing her well, walked to my home in Kirkfield Grove and punched a hole in my bathroom door. My hand hurt for about two weeks and I had to replace the door. Jean thought it was stupid of me. My only thought was that it was a shame I didn't punch Jordan; if anyone deserve a crack in the face it was him. I knew from experience that he was used to them.

"He's moping about because of some bird with big jugs that goes in the Prenton Park!" explained Sid, crassly. "They call her Funbags in there!"

"Thank you, Sid," I said, sarcastically

"Some bird with big jugs?!" Susan retorted, not impressed with Sid's lack of tact. "They call her Funbags?! Do you not think that is somewhat sexist, Sid?!"

"No!" replied Sid, nonchalantly.

"And since when have you become an expert on women's

breasts?" Susan enquired, quite clearly offended by his comments.

. "Well you can't miss hers!" he explained. "They're massive!" he added, tactlessly

Every season whenever Tranmere played any team near the Greater Manchester area Sid and me would take the opportunity to go to an away game and would spend the night at Sid's sister Susan's house. I liked Susan; she was a very nice lady. She had been my Uncle Billy's first girlfriend and I never felt she got over him. However, I always had this feeling that she secretly fancied me which was slightly worrying as she was old enough to be my mother. She would continually make suggestions that maybe I should try looking for an 'older woman' instead of chasing after 'young fillies'; she would always stick up for me and on this occasion had been asking why I was being so quiet, "Why is poor little Thomas being so quiet?" she asked, in attempt at sincerity.

So Sid explained about Katie as only Sid could, making a crass point of the fact that I hadn't 'given her one yet'.

"She sounds very nice!" Susan added with a hint of jealousy in her voice. "I do think you may be better off with an older woman though, Thomas!"

We had been going to visit Susan for a while, almost ten years now, and it always started and ended the same, and this night following the cold and extremely wet Saturday afternoon match against Stockport County was no different. After a dull 1-0 victory in a game that never got started, we took the train to Susan's house where we were greeted with a bottle of stout and a meal. Then it would start; Susan would slowly start to become suggestive towards me whilst I never knew what to say and remained quiet. Following no joy with me she would move on to Sid, wanting to know what was up with little Thomas (she always called me little Thomas, she had known me since I was a little boy); Sid, as only Sid could, would explain that I was sulking or moping, usually over some bird; at this point Susan would take offence to how Sid referred to the object of my affections, usually jumping to the poor girl's defence and always rather jealously adding the point that an older women would probably be best for me anyway. Then they would row.

Firstly, Sid would accuse her of taking my side despite the fact I usually hadn't said anything to begin with; Susan's counter would always be a reference to Sid's doomed marriage, with Sid snapping back about her knowing exactly why his marriage failed; Susan would counter this with a comment that maybe what Sid needed was a good woman himself, to which Sid would shout back that "we all know that will never happen!"; then the shrieking would begin.

They would argue, not in raised voices nor either bawling or shouting but with a series of inaudible shrieks of which they were the only two people in the world who could understand; the shrieking would end with one or both storming out of the room leaving me either on my tod or listening to one sibling slating the other sibling off. Eventually the other would return with their respective tail between their legs and then after an apology followed by a lot of hapless blubbering they would make up and be the happiest brother and sister you could ever meet.

Once they had made up Susan would get another bottle of stout out for everybody and we would all happily finish our meal. Nice home-cooked food can't beat it we all agreed. Following the completion of the meal Susan would debate whether to put on a video, then later as technology changed a DVD, of the film *A Night to Remember*. She wouldn't though. It was just a thought. Instead we would all get dragged to the sofa and following another bottle of stout Susan would get the family photo albums out and we would go through the pictures of her and Sid's parents, her and Sid as kids, her and Sid as teenagers, her and Sid as adults, my uncle Billy and their Auntie Beattie.

Reminiscent of Grandma from the Giles cartoons, Auntie

Beattie was Susan's favourite relative and as she gripped my arm tightly she would recall all her tales of Auntie Beattie adamant I had never heard the tales before. Auntie Beattie was a connoisseur of Brown ale and a wrestling enthusiast. The reason Susan had moved from Birkenhead to the outskirts of Manchester was because of Auntie Beattie; she was getting old and needed caring for because Auntie Beattie wasn't in particularly great shape either, although still lethal with a hatpin, brolly and handbag by all accounts related by the bus conductor, postman and policeman respectively. As a result Susan inherited Auntie Beattie's house and kept it in as a good a state as Auntie Beattie did herself. It was immaculate. Sid would then tell me about when he used to take Auntie Beattie to see the wrestling at Liverpool Stadium. He had never told me this tale before; well, he could never remember telling me the tale and it would always revolve around the time some big American brute that was beating on a "nice young man from Ellesmere Port". Auntie Beattie took exception to this and after leaving her ringside seat she promptly got stuck in on the American brute herself with her handbag. I would just nod and then 'ooh' then 'aaahhh!' and genuinely treat this as if I had never heard the tale before. And Susan and Sid would quite happily believe I had never heard it, despite that there were parts where I knew where to join in.

Following the tales of Auntie Beattie and her demise (her last known words were regarding who had won on the wrestling that afternoon and the result of the 2.30 at Chepstow) we would all have another bottle of stout and all head to bed. Sometimes I felt Susan would rather I went to her bed but you must remember she was a friend's sister, was old enough to be my mother and on this occasion I was pining for my lovely gorgeous Katie. Lying in a bed in the depths of Greater Manchester and being able to hear Sid snoring in the next room is not ideal but when you are in love with the world's most beautiful girl and can't stop thinking of a particular denim miniskirt it can be hell. Then there was the possibility Susan could burst into the room wearing a negligee and wanting to know if I was okay whilst inquiring if I needed the love of an older woman – I wouldn't know where to look or what to say to start with!

CHAPTER FOUR

My Family and Other Animals

The next morning Sid and I would return to Birkenhead with Sid adding to Susan that we must come to visit again soon. I found myself thinking why do I let myself go through this every time? I liked Sid, I liked Susan, but I hated being caught up in the middle of their bickering arguments like a security guard off *The Jerry Springer Show*!

Another thing I always wondered about was whether I should have a better relationship with my own two sisters. Sid might have bickered, argued and shrieked with Susan but they were mighty close. They spoke to each other on a regular basis, shared their closest secrets and problems as well as Sid having a good relationship with his nephew, Susan's son. Sid also had a decent relationship with his brother and his nieces. I can confidently state that I don't have a good relationship with my sisters. We hardly see each other and when we do we don't really speak. They both have children and I am far from the doting uncle; in fact when I hear them coming I run for cover along with Dolly but unfortunately unlike Dolly I'm not able to hide under the bed.

I'm not a child-friendly person and I've always blamed my sisters for this. My eldest sister was always fat, bossy and sarcastic, so when she brought home her first boyfriend we were all shocked. A few months later when she announced there would soon be the stomping of little bossy boots we were even more shocked. The boyfriend and father of my niece was one of the most instantly detestable people of all time; a scrawny sociology student with a big nose, he got under everyone's skin straight away with his pompous, self-absorbed personality and his loony left-wing views such as doing away with the armed forces and banning everything that could possibly cause offence. Except to the English as we were responsible for everything that had ever gone wrong on the planet, and in his world we should be offended and discriminated against as much as possible. Global warming, the ice age, hurricanes, earthquakes, Two Point Four Children and whoever thought it was a good idea to eat meat, the English were the ones to blame. Oh, meat was murder and he wasn't too enthusiastic about sport either which he had labelled as the root of all evil. None of us were sad when my bitter, sarcastic sister split up with the obnoxious twerp. But this would be a false blessing for me.

Now my eldest sister had split from this twerp there would be a custody battle; my sister ended up with custody of the brat. Every Sunday the twerp and his parents would have the brat for the day. They would always successfully return a dirty, rude, tantrum-throwing brat stuffed full of junk food to our front door adamant on having its own way. Typical of a child from a broken home the brat would manipulate what she could in a game of one-upmanship and was a spoilt brat whom no one would discipline and would be allowed to get away with murder. Oh, I did hate Sundays! I once went out with a girl who bored me senseless one Sunday just to escape the brat on her return. The movie we saw was dire, the burgers we ate afterwards were undercooked and the kiss we had at the end of the night was sloppy and cold, reminiscent of a kebab I had once had in Crewe. It still beat putting up with the brat; both the date and the kebab.

My younger sister didn't fare much better with boyfriends. I was completely horrified when she brought home a lad called Ricky who I went to school with and we called him Fatlips due to his Mick Jagger-esque tyre-tread lips. I was later relieved to find out that they never consummated their relationship; Ricky had apparently failed to rise to the occasion which I wasn't so relieved to find out about!

Anyhow, the younger sister managed to gain herself a son a

few years back following a liaison with a lad who claimed to play or to have had played for Liverpool or Everton and sometimes both; he could never remember which team though. He had also once scored for Liverpool or Everton and sometimes both; he recalled the goal he had scored once for either Liverpool or Everton and sometimes both. The goal was recalled to me by him on a number of occasions; it had been scored against three different teams, in four different positions and from six different situations but he had only scored the one goal, mind you. My younger sister, on the other hand, was miffed by the whole pregnancy situation. "How am I pregnant?" she asked in a bemused tone looking at the results of the pregnancy test, "it's not like I shared someone else's bath water!"

The boyfriend didn't last but my nephew is still going strong. It's hard to describe him; he's one of those little boys who always has a daft grin on his face and always has the look of a child who is in the process of or about to do something naughty the moment your back is turned. Ultimately, like his mother he can't do anything wrong in the eyes of his parent so therefore has never done anything wrong and could never be punished. Sometimes I wish I could be a kid again, get into trouble and not get punished. Try getting on the wrong side of the taxman and giving them a daft grin; it would be as about as useful as a condom machine in the Vatican!

That Sunday night when we came back from Susan's, I lay in my bed away from Sid's snoring wondering what it would be like if Katie ever met my family. Or what was left of them; my mother, two sisters, one niece, one nephew, an aunt and extremely annoying uncle plus a cousin or two in Southport and an estranged aunt in New Zealand. My mother can be embarrassing at the best of times with her ill-judged comments and clueless observations. One sister was bossy and sarcastic; the other naive, ignorant and clueless, a daddy's little princess who could never do anything wrong; a spoilt little madam and a naughty little boy; and an aunt I'd never met! What would they make of Katie? And what would Katie make of them?! Then would Katie wear that denim miniskirt and, most importantly, would my family like that on Katie as much as I do?!

One thing I definitely told myself was that should Katie ever meet my family then one person she would definitely not meet is my screamingly annoying cousin in Southport, Aubrey. I mean Aubrey, what type of person names their child Aubrey?! That's just asking for the kid to get ridiculed for the rest of their life. To be honest I didn't believe that people named their children Aubrey, a bit like the name Percy; I can never imagine people being named Percy. It's not used on people under the age of forty and more often reserved for annoying, unimaginative toys or cartoon pigs; I remember someone buying one of those electric pigs for the brat one year. It made a completely annoying din and drove me completely mad. But I digress.

Apparently, Aubrey was named after his paternal grandfather; many moons before my mother's sister decided to marry this screamingly annoying man that worked as a second-hand car dealer who could be a pain in the neck within minutes of talking to him, and it was he whose father was named Aubrey. After the first two children had arrived they added the dratted Aubrey a few years after I was born.

What was so bad about Aubrey you think, was it just his name? Everything was wrong with Aubrey! He was a bore, a drag and buzz killer; he didn't like playing games because they were too rough, he would rather be out skipping and jumping, he didn't like TV or radio regardless of what was on, every single book in the world seemed to be terrible, magazines were apparently for morons and he squealed with fear when he saw a video game. Aubrey instead liked to read from the Bible in order to tell everyone they were wrong and he enjoyed putting people on guilt trips. There wasn't anything anyone could enjoy without Aubrey putting them on guilt trip; have the last potato in the dish and we would be told that there are people starving in Africa. Look at something the wrong way and we would get a good dose of the 'Good Book'. Laugh at a joke and we would be told how crass, unfunny and un-politically correct it was to laugh. I kissed a girl one afternoon and was branded a perverted degenerate. Life with Aubrey was pretty dire. If you wanted a good time then forget it; if he didn't like it then no one else should. This, by the way, included Tranmere Rovers.

I remember as a kid when he went crying to his father because I had a football scarf on. I had to take it off and apologise to Aubrey because apparently Aubrey didn't like football, he had to play football at school; he found it very rough and got himself dirty. My heart bled for the poor little boy. Aubrey's father was very proud of his boy, well, he said he was. He would say how good it was to have a good Christian boy with strong morals and a generous personality who would make a fine husband for a fine woman one day, finally giving tremendous pride one day to the family. My Uncle seemed a bit oblivious to the fact that Aubrey would be highly unlikely to marry any woman on any day at any time; my grandmother once commented out loud when Aubrey was seen coming to our house one morning that she was very sure by the way he walked that he was "one of them". Apparently, Sid agreed on that one, too.

As a rule Aubrey was universally hated in my family; should we see my aunt and uncle from Southport with their darling son in tow we would run for cover. No one could stand him. That was until my youngest sister found out he was into similar interests as her; clothes and boy bands, the two of them would talk for hours. It was nice to have the little pain out of our necks for a while.

The quarter final away at Manchester City was a disaster. First of all Katie and I couldn't get tickets which had seemingly been picked up by a load of recovering amnesiacs on the Wirral Peninsula who had suddenly regained their memories and remembered that there was in fact a football team in Birkenhead called Tranmere Rovers and that they supported Tranmere. Nothing to do with the fact Tranmere were on a good FA Cup run and were also flying high at the top of League One. It was nothing to do with them being fair-weather fans, not in the slightest. They were real fans. Or so they said. So we had to watch it on TV in the pub and by we I mean Katie and I, augmented by Sid. Sid was full of his usual anecdotes and gossip, a series of half-told tales of no interest to anyone with half a brain. As a rule Sid's tales of no interest only seemed to appeal to viewers of the *Jeremy Kyle Show* and readers of *Heat* magazine. After ten minutes of hearing about the man from up the road who does things, I was far from impressed.

Then there was the game itself. Firstly Rovers had a perfectly good goal disallowed in the first ten minutes, the ref missed a blatant handball by a Man City defender, three minutes later he added insult to injury by giving City a penalty after one of their prima donnas took a dive, and the penalty was duly converted. From then on it just got worse.

A second goal was added from a spectacular overhead kick, and then Cresswell got sent off. A soft goal was given away at the beginning of the second half thanks to a weak back pass. Another perfectly good Rovers goal was disallowed before a drunken bum fell and knocked over our drinks. Rovers physio Les Parry took a tumble running out on to the pitch to tend to an injured player. A well-taken goal was added and Tranmere were out of the Cup. The final score was 4-0 to Man City. We didn't even have the pleasure of Sid spilling a half-time coffee. Probably because he didn't have one but still he could have made the effort to spill something! As long as it wasn't my drink that was spilt. Or Katie's. I had paid good money for those!

We sat at our table next to each other with our elbows on the table, our chins resting on our hands.

"That referee was shit!" said Katie.

"Tell me about it!" I agreed, "If I did my job as bad as that I'd have no business!"

"The third goal was soft!" Katie added.

I sighed, "It was a bit naff..." I murmured.

"I hope Les Parry is okay," Katie said, "that was a nasty tumble he took!"

We both sighed deeply at the same time; I could hear Sid laughing, "What are you laughing at?" I said sharply.

"You two sat there!" Sid said. "The looks on your faces with your shirts on. You're like twins! Or one of those tight-knit middle-aged couples who wear matching knitted sweaters at Chris de Burgh concerts!"

Katie looked at me and I looked at Katie; as much as we had denied it to ourselves and each other at the time, we knew we had fallen in love with each other and it was obvious to everyone. It was that exchange of looks that finally confirmed it for me. In the words of the immortal song *Plan 9, Channel 7* by The Damned, we were two hearts that were beating as one. To me it now just felt like only being a matter of time before something seriously happened between us...

"It's quite easy," I said to Katie as I placed my arm around her waist and guided her arm, "you just relax your arm and let it go!"

Katie released the dart gently and it spiralled into the single-twenty bed. "Is that okay?" Katie asked.

"It's a good start!" I smiled.

Suddenly, I looked across from the dartboard and realised that half the pub were watching us and they could see where my hand was placed on Katie. I've been playing darts for a long time, I find it relaxing, I don't take it too seriously and I enjoy it. People tell me I'm good so when Sid started telling Katie I was good at darts she insisted I teach her to play. I couldn't say no to Katie.

There we were, my arm around her, stood almost cheek to cheek discussing the rudiments of the game. And there were half the pub led by Sid staring at us with tremendous interest.

"What are you looking at?" I asked.

"I'm just watching you playing darts, Tommy!" Sid assured me with a grin.

"Are you really?" I asked not convinced.

"It's always a pleasure to watch you!" Sid told me with a daft grin.

"You can't see the board from where you're sat!" I said to him in a slightly annoyed voice. I didn't like my friendship with Katie being played out in front of the audience in the Prenton Park. Something told me that Sid had been giving everyone in the pub the full low-down on my potential relationship with Katie. When it came to gossip Sid certainly was the man! He was to gossip what Mickey was to mice!

"How long have you been playing darts?" Katie asked.

"About fourteen years now," I told her as I fired in a 140.

"Do you play any tournaments?" Katie enquired.

"No, I'm not good enough!" I laughed.

"I think you're good," Katie said with a smile, "I think you should go in for a tournament!"

I paused and found myself staring into her eyes; a compliment from a beautiful woman can go a long way, it could be a case of Alexandra Palace here I come. The pub descended into a hush as we stood there smiling at each other; suddenly we were aware of the embarrassing hush and I scuttled off to the toilets.

Only a matter of time, I told myself as I washed my hands, sooner or later it's going to happen. The question was when. A couple of problems came to mind, namely her boyfriend. Katie had told me of his violent past; I knew if anything of an adult nature was to happen then Katie must be single and I must be single. The second part wasn't too hard; I had been single for over a year and I had just about given up on love when Katie had walked into my life. The first part was difficult, Katie's boyfriend was a brutal thug who would quite happily pound her if she dared look at someone else; I knew the black eye she had suffered was a result of our kiss at the game against Liverpool.

I slipped back into the bar, amidst a few childish laughs, where I found Katie sat with Sid who was telling her at length about Hannah, an ex of mine, why she was nicknamed Frank Spencer, why he didn't like her and why the police had been around to her house the previous evening.

"I really like you, Katie!" Sid said to her with a kind smile. "I think you are perfect for him!" he added nodding in my direction.

"Sid's a nice man!" said Katie as we walked down Everest Road.

"He is," I replied, "he's been a good friend over the years!"

"How did you become friends?" she asked.

"He was a family friend, he'd come along to Rovers games with me, my dad, my grandad, my grandad's friend Harry and my Uncle Billy," I explained. "I've always viewed Sid like an uncle!"

"If he was a little younger and I was single I think I'd go out with him!" she told me.

"I think he'd be flattered but you're not his type!" I replied.

"Oh!" said Katie. "Interested in women his own age, is he?"

"Not really..." I added.

"Am I your type?" she asked after a pause.

"Yes!" I said softly.

She looked at me with a beautiful smile and a sexy glint in her eye. I wrapped my arm around her waist, she put her arm around my waist, and we continued walking on. At her building we found ourselves wrapped around each other gazing into each other's eyes; I kissed her on the cheek. "It's my birthday next week..." she began.

"I am aware," I interrupted, "it's mine, too! And Johnny King's..."

"I'm having a party at the Sailing Club," Katie continued. "I'd like you to be there!"

"That'd be grand!" I said, optimistically; right then I was longing to kiss Katie again, just like I had the day of the Liverpool game.

"You can meet Jordan!" she added.

My jaw bolted tight. "How delightful!" I muttered falsely through my clenched jaw, the desire to kiss suddenly gone.

"I'm sure you'll be great friends!" she advised me.

I headed home. I paid my Rock Ferry Tobacco Duty to a pensioner who was a bit worse for wear. He asked me what was wrong and why I had such a long face. I proceeded to explain that I was in love with a girl who was in love with me but who was the girlfriend of a complete penis. He smoked one cigarette while I explained the situation; he told me I had better give him another and a spare one for later and that would probably help resolve everything. I went on home. But one thing ran through my mind; how was I to tell Katie I thought I already knew Jordan? But even more importantly, and very disturbingly, how I knew him...

I've always met parties with an element of mistrust. From those early days of being invited around on a school-friend's birthday for a few ridiculous and tedious party games and a tasteless buffet, to those drunken adult parties where nobody leaves the kitchen and I'm one of those people who hovers around the back door smoking endless cigarettes and discussing how bad a party it is. Name a bad party experience and I have had it. I once got talked into going to a Halloween party about three years ago. I only went because I was hoping a young lady would be there and it might be the start of something special. It wasn't, as the said young lady was never invited to the party and the party never really got started; it was all over by eleven o'clock. I ended up in a lousy nightclub drinking warm, flat lager. Jesus wept.

Few good things have ever happened at parties for me; I'm

usually the type of person that fails to meet anyone, has a lousy time and no one seems to notice once they have gone. On the odd occasion I've got into a scrap with some idiot. However, I did have success at one party though; myself and a nice young lady had a special moment in a discreet bedroom. I had turned up that evening full of dread and absolutely no optimism in the forthcoming evening wondering why I had got talked into this. After a couple of awkward drinks and a smoke outside the back door I was ready to do one and head home. Thankfully, just as I was contemplating my escape the said young lady slipped out of the back door, our eyes met and we started a conversation; we headed back inside and spent the rest of the evening chatting in the lounge. It was one of those parties where everyone, as usual, seemed to be in the kitchen so they didn't notice when we slipped upstairs for a bit of how's your father. We parted with the promise to call each other but we never did; we were simply ships that passed in the night; her name was Katie, too. I think.

When Katie told me of her plans to hold a party I was filled with fear; I could imagine this ending in disaster. I would turn up be introduced to a few people who wouldn't say another word to me during the whole evening and then when I left the party no one would notice, most notably Katie. That was unless I managed to get into a scrap with Jordan in front of Katie's family and friends. Then I could imagine my popularity would be up there with a group of Jehovah's Witnesses turning up at a wife-swapping party; and not adventurous Jehovah's Witnesses either, they would be the type who wanted to tell you about the Good News and the Lord's Message. I recalled the previous party I had attended.

It had been well over a year since I had been to a party of any description and then it had been quite an experience. I was in the last throws of a relationship with my ex Hannah and the company she worked for was having an office party. For some reason she decided that I needed to be invited; why, I'm not exactly sure but I have surmised that Hannah had advised her colleagues that our relationship was on the rocks and she wanted her colleagues to see what she might be throwing away. I have a feeling she would have described me as some big, fat, football fan with no sense of fashion or style and a crap job who liked to use a lot of long fancy words.

Even though I wore a smart shirt and turned up well presented, I had a sense of dread; I dreaded that all Hannah's colleagues were going to be awfully stuck up people who looked at the common man with distaste. Actually, Hannah's colleagues were alright, they were neither stuck-up nor looked at me with distaste. In fact, the only person who looked at me with distaste or was stuck-up towards me was Hannah herself. Oh, she did enjoy waltzing around and describing me as a great embarrassment as well as being uncultured and a non-intellectual. So I did what anyone else would do in a similar situation and slowly got drunk. One of the people she had introduced me to was her manager, a rather attractive Canadian lady in her early forties who was very well endowed in the chest area. After Hannah had hit me with a barrage of abuse she then introduced me to her manager and I kind of proceeded to hit it off with her manager.

Hannah made the mistake of introducing her manager to me as being an American. That is a big mistake to a Canadian, just as it is when accusing someone from Birkenhead of being from Liverpool. It's like an awkward child or a dodgy curry; it doesn't sit too well. I've always been very defensive of Birkenhead, and in particular, Rock Ferry; neither are exactly the worst places in the world to live and when somebody accuses me of being from Liverpool it really grinds my gears. You know that horrid sound your car makes when you don't quite get the clutch in when trying to change gears; well that's the type of sound I make internally when I get accused of being from Liverpool. When the lovely Canadian lady was accused of being American I knew how she felt and I could see that her gears were grinding.

Anyhow, myself and the attractive older woman hit it off quite well and, as mentioned, at some point we kind of disappeared for a bit of a kiss and a cuddle in one of the office storerooms. Common sense prevailed that night and I went home feeling worse for wear whilst listening to Hannah's lecture on what an embarrassment I was because I had no sense of fashion, was pretty stupid and spent my night talking to the sad old office tart. If only she knew.

If only she did know; it was a week or so later on New Year's Day when our relationship was thankfully terminated. I let the dust settle and two weeks later I took a box of Hannah's belongings to her workplace with the intent of returning them to her. Her rather increasingly attractive manager greeted me, advised that Hannah was on an extended lunch break and promised to ensure they were returned to her as soon as possible. Simple enough, you would think, box of belongings returned and that's it. Only there was a spanner in the works. Hannah's manager asked if I could give her a lift home; her car was at the garage and she hated getting the bus and taxis were far too expensive so I happily complied all too easily.

When we got to the rather lovely Canadian lady's home, I wasn't surprised that she asked me in to have a look at a dripping tap in the kitchen that simply had to be looked at. Once again I happily complied and happily repaired her tap for her; the offer of a cup of tea was greeted with enthusiasm and whilst the lady in question prepared the tea, I went to clean up. Changing the washer on a tap can be quite messy. When I returned to the kitchen I was not shocked to find my Canadian hostess with her foot on the kitchen table chair adjusting her stocking. "How about it?" she asked me as I gazed on at her fine legs with admiration. Certainly a Mrs Robinson incident! Nevertheless I readily complied once more.

I would have stayed with my Canadian hostess a little longer but the threat of her husband coming home any minute forced me to make a quick exit and she advised that if she ever needed a plumbing job done again she would give me a call. I certainly had plenty to think about on my drive back home to Rock Ferry through the busy rush-hour traffic that evening.

I couldn't imagine such an incident at Katie's party but then again I never imagined the chain of events that would be set off the last time I was at a party. I did wonder though, why didn't my lovely Canadian lady ever drop me a bell when she needed a plumbing job doing again? I always thought I was a pretty good plumber...

CHAPTER FIVE

How to Deal with Bullies

I was having a real dilemma; all week I was trying to decide whether I should go to Katie's party. I knew Jordan would be there and I might not be able to control my temper around him but I didn't want to let Katie down. My own personal agony aunt Jean told me the best thing to do was go; Katie wanted me to be there for her. Plus, Jean added, it would be a chance for Katie to compare me against her rotten boyfriend. Sid recalled the time when we got stuck in Milton Keynes when we went to watch a match; we thought it would be terrible but as it turned out it wasn't that bad. We found a nice pub with nice people and ended up having a great night. It was decided, for Katie's sake, I would go.

That evening I walked down to the sailing club with a replica Tranmere away shirt for Katie (she always said she wanted one) and a false sense of optimism. Katie had booked a karaoke, so I thought I could impress her with some singing; I'm not one to blow my trumpet but I've got one hell of a voice. Many moons before, my fat, sarcastic sister had taunted me after her own singing at a karaoke nearly cleared a venue; she told me it was better than I could do, no one would want to listen to me sing and I couldn't sing to begin with. After I belted out the classic hit *Eloise* by The Damned she still said I couldn't sing but the people who had flocked back disagreed with her! Never mind, eh?

I met Katie's family and friends; they were very nice people, they took to me well and I kind of got the feeling they preferred me more to a certain other person. There were people there I liked and a couple of people I didn't. Then I finally met Jordan, well I was formally introduced to him. If you've not already twigged, Jordan was my earlier acquaintance on Bedford Avenue the days of the York and Liverpool games. Within two minutes I loathed him even more; I tried to remain cordial with him but I couldn't knowing what he'd done to Katie. Jordan got under my skin very easily; he had what I call Aaron Noonan complex.

Aaron Noonan is a local nuisance, a pizza delivery man by trade, a magnet for trouble in reality; nothing is ever his fault or so he claims. Getting barred from a pub for being annoying and causing countless people to leave whilst nursing a glass of still orange all night, it's not his fault, it's everyone else's fault. Getting a parking ticket for parking on double yellow lines, not his fault, it's the traffic wardens picking on him; being banned from a public library for continually using a mobile phone in there, not his fault, the librarian's not realising his absolute need to use it. Getting in trouble with the local council about the stockpile of rubbish outside his house, not his fault, the rubbish is in fact very valuable in particular the sodden cardboard boxes that can no longer be used in any shape or form; following through on the number 15 bus after eating out-of-date pâté, not his fault, it was an accident. Aaron Noonan is a man who can get under your skin quickly by talking complete rubbish and trying to insist he's right when he is clearly wrong. Another thing about Noonan is that he's always believes he's right even when he's wrong, and even when he's been proven wrong he'll still be able to insist he is right. He's a self-appointed expert on everything, in particular music. I once made the fatal mistake of pointing out that Al Martino's number one hit *Here In My Heart* was the first ever UK number one; Noonan on the other hand insisted, insisted and insisted that it was *Spanish Eyes*. He promptly told me I knew nothing and wouldn't know about things like that anyway; even when I produced the Guinness book of hits, he still insisted he was right and I was wrong! I half expected him to write to the Guinness book of hits to tell them they were wrong...

The man's personal hygiene is questionable at best: a man who washes once a month, a man who buys his clothes from a charity shop then throws them away once dirty so he doesn't have to wash them. This is a man who can clear any given venue at any given time with just his mere presence. One of his little lectures consisted of running down a local pub verbally because it was apparently unclean and untidy; it costs nothing to be clean was his statement. Pot, kettle and black were the words that came to mind.

Jordan struck me as being like Aaron Noonan because nothing seemed to be his fault: his criminal record; his unemployment; his ignorance; his attitude; it was all the fault of everyone else, the government, his family, the schools, society and most of all Katie. All night he kept sucking up to me, trying to act like my friend, offering me drinks all whilst running Katie down behind her back. I hated him, especially the way he treated Katie, the horrid way he spoke to her; he called her fat, thick and useless but none of that was true. It made my gears grind. I was stood at the bar when he slunk over, "Fancy a drink?" he asked in a greasy voice.

"No," I said bluntly, not wishing to converse with him.

"I can't believe I had to come here for that stupid bitch!" he snarled. "I could be off screwing this bird I know! Right filthy slag she is, she'll do anything! Want her number?"

"I'll pass on that one!" I told Jordan with an element of contempt.

"I mean Katie is a right frigid bitch!" Jordan claimed. "Shagging her is like shagging a bag of sand!"

"Please don't speak about her like that!" I said firmly.

He snarled at me, "Where do I know you from?" he asked with a sudden change of tack. "Do you know Lee McGurnigan?"

"You keep trying to bum cigarettes off me on Bedford Avenue!" I replied sharply.

"Do I?" he replied innocently. "When did I do that?"

"A number of times," I began, "like the day Rovers beat Liverpool in the Cup!"

"Did I? I had to give her a slap that day," he snarled, "I saw her snogging some prick at the game on the TV! Stupid bitch, isn't she?!"

My blood began to boil once more. "Be careful how you treat her!" I warned him in a calm voice.

"Do you fancy her?!" he snarled.

"I care about her!" I told him.

"Keep your hands off her! That's my property!" he sneered, arrogantly. "If you touch her I'll break your teeth and I'll give her a kicking, too, for good measure!"

"Is that so?!" I asked without intimidation.

"Watch it, tosser, I've bottled people for less!" he threatened.

"I know you have," I replied calmly I moved closer and whispered, "You bottled me, didn't you? Clifton Park wasn't it? For no good reason, wasn't it?!"

"I had a reason!" growled Jordan.

"What the hell did I do to deserve that?!" I demanded. "What did I do to you to deserve that?"

"I can't think of a reason but you were disrespecting me," Jordan answered, "that was the act of a disrespected man!"

"That was the act of a gutless coward if you ask me and I hate cowards!" I replied, incensed. "You wouldn't know what respect is! How do you know what disrespect is when you don't know anything about respect?" I asked, angrily. I stared him in the eye, "I gave you the kicking of your life because of what you did! How are your ribs these days?"

Straight away Jordan backed down; I could tell I'd intimidated him. When you stand up to a bully you can be sure that pretty soon you'll meet a coward. A little while later Jordan disappeared off with a girl called Jessica; she was a supposed friend of Katie's, I thought she was just plain obnoxious. She was self-absorbed, fickle and neither attractive physically nor personality wise. I decide to settle down with Katie and I told her how beautiful she was, all the things she needed to hear especially after the way that thug had spoken to her and how he'd treated her. Jordan's attitude to Katie just stank, the way he called her stupid and made out she was a criminal because she worked at bank were just plain obnoxious. What really ground my gears were the comments he made when he described her as being a "Tits for Brains": the type of woman who has two main assets but very little else personality and intelligence wise. I hated to see Katie being treated as nothing more than a large pair of breasts. Katie was so much more than that. It was wonderful to see her beautiful smile as I poured compliments on her. I got up on the karaoke and belted out *You've Lost That Lovin' Feeling* by the Righteous Brothers as Katie smiled on. Katie cheered the hardest of anyone once I'd finished.

Katie's mother came over to speak to her so I took the opportunity to nip outside for a smoke. And it was then that I just happened to wander around the wrong corner at the wrong time. And there was Jordan with Jessica – having a quickie. I really didn't need to see that! I thought they had gone! I slipped back into the club quickly; I was feeling flustered. Then the first person I saw was Katie; what do I say? Nothing, I thought, no, I should, no, it's not my place, and what should I do? Moments later Jordan barged in with Jessica; from the look on Katie's face I knew she suspected something. Jordan had acquired a small flat bottle of vodka from somewhere and he was drinking it straight from the bottle. A member of staff tried to take the bottle off him but he verbally abused him, then he turned on Katie. I glared at him, he backed off. I walked over to Katie, "Are you okay?" I asked quietly.

She nodded; I could see she was threatened by him. I'm not sure what happened next, it just happened so quickly. Jordan started beating Katie's uncle for no apparent reason, he had just dragged him off a seat and began to beat him. Next thing Jordan picked up a stool and hurled it at the bar smashing all the optics and scaring a lot of people half to death. He was restrained by the security, the police were called and shortly after he was carted off, f-ing and blinding about how it was everyone else's fault, especially Katie's, to the nick in the back of a scallywagon. Katie fell into shock; she remained chatty cheerful, friendly and outgoing but deep down I knew she was hurting and I could see she was reining in the pain, the humiliation and the shock of the whole incident. She went around to everyone, her family and friends, the staff, me, the man doing the karaoke and apologised for Jordan's actions; she said it wasn't his fault; he had anger issues and was seeing a psychiatrist. The only thing I thought it could be was Aaron Noonan Complex. That or he was vile, cowardly, a thug who needed taking down a peg. I would quite happily do that once again.

When the last two people left were Katie and me, I decided it was time to phone a taxi. I went back to her flat with her, we walked in the door and it was then that she broke down in tears. I held her, helped her to the couch, gave her a shoulder to cry on and dried her tears. I heated up some chicken and noodle soup for her, and then we cuddled up in bed. We began to talk; Tranmere, Johnny King, love. We kissed a few times and I told her how beautiful she was and how amazing I thought she was. We didn't have sex. Later she asked me why I didn't ask or try; I told her she was vulnerable and I wasn't going to take advantage of her in that condition. I had too much respect for Katie plus I thought that thug might hurt her again if we did. We kissed some more. Around 6.30 a.m. Katie thanked me for looking after her but she wanted to go to sleep. Wrapped in a blanket she saw me to the door where we kissed just like we had on the day of the Cup game against Liverpool. "Thank you for looking after me, Tommy," she said. "You've been a real friend; I really enjoyed your singing, too." We kissed again. "By the way," she added, "Happy Birthday, Tommy!"

With three games to go Tranmere were at the top of League One and one glorious Friday night in late April we needed a win against Brentford to secure both promotion to the Championship and the League One title.

I walked with Katie hand in hand to the ground in silence. I could tell something was up but I didn't ask, she would tell me when she was ready; her silence wasn't really that worrying, it was more curious. She kept glancing across at me and smiling deeply. We had developed an amazing bond; it felt at times we could read each other's minds. We could read each other's body language so well and we knew how each other felt without having to ask. Since our joint birthdays two weeks earlier I could tell that sooner or later something would happen between us; from our conversations I could tell she wanted to split from Jordan. She was no longer defending him, she would speak of the embarrassment he caused, how his behaviour upset her and that she suspected he was cheating on her. A couple of days before I'd received a threatening phone call, an aggressive chav telling me to keep away from his bird or he would have me knifed. I knew it was Jordan. Jordan got told, though, if there is one thing I've ever learnt from life it is never back down to bullies.

As a youngster I only ever went to The Dell Primary School in Rock Ferry; it was okay I suppose. I could tolerate infant and junior school. Just about tolerate, by the way, I was never particularly enthusiastic about school; I was always very dubious of anyone who said they enjoyed school. I found school boring and pointless at the best of times! The worst telling off I ever got as a kid was the time I announced one Sunday lunchtime that I didn't like school. "What do you mean you don't like school?!?!" I was bellowed at by all and sundry staring at me as if I had just announced my conversion to devil-worshipping or worse, That Bloody Stretford Mob; my older sister didn't help by adding in her creepiest and crawliest kiss-up voice that she liked school. I tried justifying that I hated school because I had to get out of bed at a ridiculous time in the morning, had to wear a horrid school uniform with a stupid and extremely pointless tie, found all the lessons boring, detested the eternally pointless hymn practice and didn't like the boy I had to sit next to during lunchtimes. What I didn't tell all and sundry, as my sister announced how much she loved her school uniform and getting out of bed in the morning was the highlight of her day as well as loving all lessons and, in particularly, hymn practice, was that it was the bullies I really detested. And to my sister's credit she advised all and sundry that no one liked the boy I had to sit next to during lunchtimes!

My experience of bullies went back to my very first day at school; I recall on that very first break time my shoe slipping off and the big ugly thug with the peculiar-shaped head two years older than me began to kick it around the playground with his friends like at football. It was my own fault. Or so I was told. You should have your shoes tied up, said the teacher. You should stay away from those boys, said my sister. Can't trust you with anything, said my mother.

Sometimes with bullies you never know what exactly you have done wrong but you have done something wrong. Most of my time was spent with the same two mouth pieces calling me 'Monkey Face' at school; why I don't know, why they chose me I don't know and what I had done to earn their wrath I haven't got the foggiest! Every time I turned around they were there ready to give me abuse; I even once asked them why they did it and they told me. "Because we don't like you!"

Fair enough, I thought. "Why don't you like me?" I asked.

"We just don't, okay?!" they replied.

After a while of being labelled 'Monkey Face' I became distinctly fed up of it. Being eight years old I felt the correct course of action would be to tell my mother. "Don't tell lies!" she barked at me, and told me, "I know those boys' mothers and they would never do that!"

Great help you are, I thought – from that moment I learnt that without a shadow of a doubt grown-ups and in particular your parents could not be relied on for anything, especially your mother and especially when trying to tackle bullies!

Parents make you do the strangest things, too; like making you join the cub scouts. Why was I made to join the cub scouts? I hated the cub scouts! I found it tedious and pointless; it was good training in wussiness skills though. Meet any world-class wussy and you can guarantee they have been involved in the scout movement all the way through the ranks. You know the type; weak, dull, gutless and cowardly.

"All your friends go!" my mother advised me when I protested at being sent to a freezing cold church hall in Rock Ferry every Wednesday evening.

Fair enough, I thought, a number of my friends were cub scouts, too. But so were all the bullies from school and a nice new pile of people I would grow to loathe such as the smelly kid named Mark Challis who always mouthed off at me for no reason. It meant that after being called Monkey Face all week I would be subjected to it one night of the week as well. Plus, I would miss out on one night's TV. No *Dr Who* for me on Wednesdays...

"It'll be good for you!" I was told by my mother. Why do parents insist they know what is best for their children? Being addressed as Monkey Face never did me any good! I remember when I was forced against my will to go to the pack camp with the advice that I would love it and it would be so much fun that when I was collected I wouldn't want to go home; the omens weren't good when one of my bullies was placed in the same dorm as me. Thankfully he kicked up such a stink because he hated me so much he was moved elsewhere. A weekend of baked beans, plastic cutlery, freezing tents, the cold, heavy rain and being called Monkey Face somewhere in the depths of Cheshire was not my idea of fun! I couldn't wait to get home; I belted straight into the backseat of the car the moment it pulled up and the first thing I did when I got home was to go and barricade myself in my bedroom. Of that weekend I had one pleasant memory – Ricky Fatlips the school bully getting punched by my friend Gareth; Ricky had been part of the pack from when I joined, he was the same age as me and enjoyed pushing people around. He was given the Fatlips moniker due to the fact he had a set of tyre-tread lips Mick Jagger would have been envious of; I think I've mentioned him, haven't I? Anyhow, Ricky was a fine example of the phrase that behind every bully there is a coward; when someone stood up against him he would inevitably end up in tears and it was always Ricky's. I always believed that the cub scouts and later sea scouts gave Ricky the edge of wussiness that made him a coward.

I escaped the cub scouts not long after I turned ten never to return before any real wussiness had set in; the threat of making me a sea scout was terrifying and how exactly I managed to get out of going to cub scouts escapes me but I did. If I had remained one of 'them' I'd never have become the man I am today. I could have possibly become an over-the-top health-and-safety executive or a lino salesman or something as equally weak and anal retentive.

It's a shame Martin was never a cub scout. Martin was a childhood friend of my older sister's and from the age of 4 till I was 17 he was my bully. My first memory of Martin was him swinging me around the living room by my hair whilst he laughed like a drain as I cried in pain.

"Stay with Martin," said my mother on the first day of school, "he'll take care of you!"

Take care of me he did; he took care of the name calling, the kicking, the punching and the spreading of lies. I would frequently have to lie to explain my bruises; countless times I had to reassure my parents, teachers and even the police that I didn't take or deal drugs, indulge in depraved sexual acts with corpses or farm animals or that I had AIDS. Yes, AIDS – this rotten piece of work went around telling everyone I had AIDS; he said I'd confided in him and he had then told as many people as possible because he was 'concerned'. He was just spreading lies but what really upset me was that people believed him. Eventually, Martin got what was coming to him and I must say that Greek dentist did a fantastic job on his teeth and his falsies. Even Martin's mother thought so. What boggled her mind the most was how anyone could do such damage to their own teeth by slipping on dog dirt. Well, it would be a bit hypocritical of Martin to grass on me after all those threats he'd given me about killing me if I told anybody about the beatings he dealt me.

A rule that applied to just about everything was not to force things. I remembered a crass builder dubbed Windy due to a certain bodily function he liked to share with everyone and then brag about it afterwards. Well, that was until one afternoon he tried to force the certain bodily function and got more than he desired from the bodily function which from that day on led him to become known as Ploppy. I knew if I wanted to have a love affair with Katie then I shouldn't force it. I would just let it evolve over time; for man did not evolve from apes overnight; Millwall fans prove that some are still evolving from apes.

Once in Prenton Park Katie came to life, we spoke about Ian Goodison's rock-solid defence, Savage and Shuker's goal tally, Joe Collister's excellent form, and how it was like the Johnny King era once again. Through the game we gave our running commentary: we commentated on a bad challenge; the ref getting hit in the head by the ball; Sid spilling his half-time coffee, as usual; a Goodison clearance that cleared the Johnny King Stand and ended up on Borough Road. The longer the game went on though, the longer Brentford held us. Our commentary reduced; slowly it looked like we would have to wait until the midweek game against Leyton Orient to seal the title and promotion. When Brentford struck the bar with fifteen minutes to go we heard numerous murmurs begin to reverberate around Prenton Park that the Rovers could end up blowing both the title and promotion. Memories of New Year's Day in 1995 came to mind when we were flying high at the top of the First Division and a home defeat to bottom of the table Notts County sent us into free fall before we crashed out of the play-offs at the hands of Reading.

On 87 minutes the Brentford keeper, who had been as solid as a rock all game, spilled the ball badly from a tame shot; it squirmed around the outside of the post and the Rovers had won a corner in extremely tenuous fashion. The tension in the stand could have been cut with a knife, everywhere I looked there were nervous fans staring on; Katie's hand slipped into mine. Alan Mahon lined up the corner, it felt like hours before he struck it, the ball swung in. I can still remember what happened next as if it was yesterday. It all seemed to happen in slow motion, as the ball swung in it appeared to hang in the air for an eternity; Ian Goodison rose at the back post, his head made perfect contact with the ball, the ball hit the underside of the bar before it bounced down and then up before it dropped into the back of the net. It was 1-0 to Tranmere. The ground erupted, I hugged Katie, and Sid hugged both of us.

Brentford kicked off and nearly scored; the next three minutes felt like three hours. I thought I was going to have a fit when five minutes of added time was announced. If it hadn't been for a fine save from Joe Collister it would have all been curtains. Finally the ref blew the whistle; Sid hugged and kissed both me and Katie. Instinctively I wrapped my arms around Katie, suddenly I found myself staring into Katie's eyes, she smiled her beautiful smile and I smiled at Katie then, almost instinctively, once more I stroked away a stray hair or two before we embraced and then kissed. The look in her eyes then the mouthed words that followed said it all, "I love you."

CHAPTER SIX

Love Comes to Rock Ferry

We just lay there, cuddled up next to one another in bed. The curtains were not drawn and the moonlight shone in through the window; I gently rubbed my hands over Katie's soft beautiful naked body. By the moonlight she looked even more beautiful, like the sun setting over the River Dee in the middle of summer. When we made love it was amazing; so gentle, so passionate; we knew exactly the right areas on each other's bodies; we seemed to know exactly what the other wanted.

"You know I've split up with Jordan," Katie said after a while.

"I guessed so," I said not lifting my head from the pillow, "you wouldn't have asked me to make love to you otherwise."

I cuddled her closer. I gently stroked her hair. "How was I?" she asked quietly.

"Amazing..." I said. "How was I?"

She rested her head on my chest. "Gorgeous..." she said softly.

After the game, we'd gone to the Prenton Park; we mixed with another group of fans. We had three pints for a change, we had a game of darts which Katie won two to one and then left. We walked to my house in silence, I paid my Rock Ferry Tobacco Duty to a couple of drunks and we headed on. We reached the door to my home and Katie led me in. Katie said nothing, she simply took me by the hand and then led me up to the bedroom where we kissed by the doorway and then Katie walked into the bedroom; she sat down on the bed and told me she wanted me to make love to her. The rest was now beautiful history.

"What happened between you and Jordan then?" I asked, wondering what had triggered their split.

"He cheated on me," she said not moving her head. "I took an afternoon off work and when I got home I caught him in my bed in my flat with my so-called friend, Jessica!"

"How did you feel?" I asked curiously.

"At first I felt angry, betrayed but then I realised," Katie turned over so she was lying against me, "I could be with you!" She smiled beautifully before kissing me, "I can be with a man who really loves me, who cares about me, who really appreciates me!"

"So who would that be?" I asked with a smile.

Katie smiled, "Do you know I saw Sid in the chemists this afternoon?" she said, changing the subject.

"That doesn't surprise me, he tends to go in there a lot, it's one of his favourite haunts," I advised her. "He doesn't buy anything unless he has one of his prescriptions for one of his ailments; he likes to go in for a good gossip and see who is buying what so he can have a good gossip about that!"

"I thought he might have told you what I had been buying..." Katie said with slight smile.

"And what was that?" I asked.

"Condoms!" said Katie, bluntly. "He wouldn't get lost so I hung around for twenty minutes before I could buy them."

"He didn't say a word to me..." I told Katie. "I would have been the first person to find out if he had seen you, quickly followed by half of Birkenhead..."

Katie smiled. "I've been looking forward to this all week," she explained. "I wanted it to be special, I decided if we won tonight then tonight was the night so I bought the condoms just in case; I'm so glad we finally made love..."

We kissed some more. "Shall we again?" I asked gently rubbing my hands on her beautiful torso.

"Oh yes..." she replied, softly.

We made love and then talked some more and made love some more until the early hours. One thing we talked about was our lovers; Katie didn't want any secrets, she wanted us to be honest with each other; she told me about the men she had dated

– married men too scared to be seen with her, petty criminals ready to rip her off and men who were just plain jerks in general. She told me of the wimps she had dated such as a wet blanket who enjoyed knitting and brought it with him on dates, a mime artist with a fear of intimacy, an uber sensitive philosophy student and a mummy's boy who brought his mother on dates because he had to be home by nine o'clock. I told her about some of my exes: Lynda who I've already spoken about; Rachael a girl who was ashamed to be seen with me; Natalie, a compulsive liar, Fiona, an older woman with a drink problem and Hannah who didn't like to play second fiddle to Tranmere Rovers.

I had split from Hannah about a year before I met Katie; Hannah hated football, she called it pointless and a big waste of money; I wouldn't have minded but her favourite TV show at the time was *Big Brother*. She hated it when I went to Saturday's matches, she would sooner I traipsed round Liverpool buying her clothes she would never wear. She hated the Prenton Park pub; she would rather hang out in an anal-retentive coffee shop or a wine bar full of fakes and phonies. Throughout our relationship she constantly referred to Tranmere as my bitch. Hannah acted as if I was cheating on her when I went to matches: "You think more of that football club than you do of me!" she would say bitterly before I left for the ground on match day. Jean had the nickname of Frank Spencer for her as she always seemed to wear a black beret. We split when I went to watch Tranmere versus Southend on New Year's Day than rather watch the Christmas special of *Eastenders* for the third time.

I lay in bed with Katie as the sun rose that Saturday morning; it was a beautiful red colour as it rose over the Mersey that morning. Its beautiful, fiery colour symbolised the new dawn in my life; shortly after we both drifted off to sleep. I awoke a few hours later; I slipped out of bed and headed downstairs. I fed Dolly who was sat by the fridge door with a pathetic look on her little face as if she had never been fed in her whole life, no one loved her and she would go to the RSPCA with tales of drunk-enness and cruelty. Once the cat was fed and she was my best friend in the whole wide world again, I made myself a cup of tea and sat down to watch some TV. I put on *Sky Sports News*; they were covering Tranmere's victory from the previous night. They spoke to the players, the manager, the chairman, and the fans. They replayed the action, the nerve-jangling moments, the breathtaking near chances, the frustrating almost moments, the glorious goal, the ecstasy of the final whistle. As they replayed that glorious moment, they had caught the special moment I had shared with Katie in the Johnny King Stand. Then they showed our moment when we knocked Liverpool out of the Cup. Katie and I had become minor celebrities.

I returned upstairs to bed; to my gorgeous girl. Fewer things looked so beautiful than Katie lain asleep in my bed that morning. I do recall in the early to mid-eighties when I was about four or five and the first school trip I went on. I remember as the bus approached the Kingsway tunnel, we could see the length of the Mersey on that beautiful spring morning with the sun shining on to the Mersey and in particular I recall the trademark orange and black funnels of the Isle of Man Steam Packet Company ferries. That was beautiful.

As I slipped back under the duvet and as I began to wrap my arms against her soft, warm body she awoke and greeted me with a kiss and a beautiful smile. I told her about the TV coverage and the fact we were now minor celebrities; by the end of the year we would probably end up on celebrity reality TV maybe with our own football chat show on local cable TV. People would now think we were an item, I added, so I asked her to be my girlfriend. She smiled her beautiful smile and looked on with her kind, gorgeous eyes before whispering, "Yes!"

The very first date we had was at the Italian restaurant on Prenton Road the very next evening. Nice food, not too dear, plus the company was great. Ian Goodison, the hero of Friday's game, was at the restaurant. We exchanged pleasantries after he recognised us as the kissing couple they showed on the TV. He was pleased to be a key instigator in the beginning of our romance. I told Katie I hoped our love would last forever. She hoped it would, too.

Having a girlfriend who likes football and supports the same club as you is a blessing. My previous girlfriend, Hannah, as I mentioned didn't like football; on the one occasion I took her to a game at her insistence it was a nightmare. She complained it was cold, she didn't want to be near Sid because he wasn't wearing designer clothes, nor were the players; running around the pitch getting sweaty was disgusting, she added; sweating was apparently unhealthy according to Hannah. I tried to explain that sweating was natural and it was in fact not showering or bathing afterwards and trying to cover the sweat up with spray-on deodorants that was disgusting. She complained when I went to the toilet because it was dirty in there, she thought it was rude for the players to challenge for the ball, felt it would be nice for the other team to be allowed to score, thought the ref had no style or fashion sense and believed it was completely unfair that two people were allowed to handle the ball. Hannah also regarded all things Super and White as her love rival.

That was another thing, Hannah gave me grief over my Tranmere scarf – because it said Super White Army she was convinced I was a member of the Ku Klux Klan. Her anal-retentive friends from the anal-retentive coffee shop and the equally anally-retentive wine bar were horrified and even reported me to the police as a racist. It was all extremely embarrassing when the police turned up and after I was cleared of any misdemeanours, they were all still convinced I was a white supremacist despite my argument that Tranmere have had plenty of black and Asian players and my listing Vivian Richards, Paul Lim and Daley Thompson as my sporting heroes. Pity they didn't understand sports or the like, though. The worst thing about

Hannah was she had double standards; she would bleat on about minorities and how badly they were treated. However, when she met someone from a minority she would be completely offensive, harping on in stereotypes, talking down to people and showing a very blinkered view.

I know a Muslim electrician, Aleem, who I ask to help me out if I need electrical work done; electrics and water don't mix well so it's handy for a plumber to know an electrician. On this occasion though I had a fault in my kitchen so he came round to sort out the electrics for me. When he arrived I introduced him to Hannah. Hannah spoke to him as if he was hard of hearing and his first language was a dialect known by a remote tribe in the rainforests of New Guinea; she said how it was perfectly acceptable for his people to want to blow up innocent people because that's part of their culture, just like the Scots celebrating Burns night or the Irish celebrating St Patrick's. I asked if that's why Americans acted like arseholes because it was part of their culture. Hannah then reminded me in a high-and-mighty tone that she was part American. I didn't ask which part but I'm sure you can guess which area I would have suggested. She kept harping on how she hated bacon and that she never drank, well except for wine but no one has ever suffered from a drink-related problem as a result of wine, only the gutter classes had drink problems. Hannah then started to bang on that it must be difficult to do a job for a racist nut like me who would probably have him hung from the nearest tree if he made a mistake with the electrics or stoned to death if he refuted Christianity and all its vices despite the fact that Hannah knew I was an atheist and didn't attend church. On his way out Aleem simply asked who the loony was and was she out on day release. Enough said.

When I finally split from Hannah all my friends and family said how happy they were that we had split up and they all added that they wouldn't miss her. I remember the distinct sound of insincerity in Sid's voice when he said how sad he was that I'd split from Hannah, a bit like the time he saw a squashed seagull in the middle of Borough Road. "Oh dear, a poor squashed seagull!" he had said in an extremely insincere voice. Sid didn't get along with Hannah; he didn't like her constantly implying he was fond of ballet and that he enjoyed Michael Barrymore because he was 'You know...' Dolly was probably the happiest, I'm quite sure she deliberately defecated in her French headwear on purpose. Funny thing is I had never had Dolly down as a *Some Mothers Do 'Ave 'Em* fan; I always thought her more of a *Fawlty Towers* type cat...

As much of a pain that Hannah was there is nothing worse than having a girlfriend who claims to like football; it is far worse than a girlfriend who doesn't like football. With a football-hating girlfriend you know where you stand, it's a no-no in conversation, you're constantly told no one cares, who plays for who is irrelevant, who is who is not important and most importantly they couldn't care less and it's a load of rubbish so don't even think about putting it on TV because *Coronation Street* is on in five minutes. A girlfriend who claims to like football on the other hand is a complete liability.

My previous girlfriend to Hannah was Natalie, a girl who couldn't tell the truth; even on the odd occasion when she did get it right. It took Natalie two months to tell me when she lost her job and everything she told me about herself always seemed to contradict something she had already told me, like the time she was telling me about the wonderful holidays she had had in Thailand, then a couple of weeks later she admitted to have never having had a passport and the most exotic place she had ever been was Bournemouth. Or there was the time she told me she went to an FA Cup final at Wembley which was revealed as drivel when she admitted that the first live match she ever been to was with me at Prenton Park. Oh dear. Natalie told me she loved football and was an Arsenal fan. Well, she owned an Arsenal shirt and occasionally watched them on TV when they showed highlight clips on the news. There is nothing worse than a know nothing fair-weather fan telling a dedicated fan of a smaller club that the club they claim to support is so much better than the dedicated fan's team. Sid said on numerous occasions he could have throttled her due to her prattle. Natalie kept asking why I supported a shit football team and then said I should become an Arsenal fan so it wouldn't be so embarrassing for me. One afternoon she took me to a sports shop so I could buy myself an Arsenal shirt and scarf. She couldn't fathom that I chose to support Tranmere, because they are my local team who I've followed for three decades, not because they've won some titles and are up near the top of the league. On one occasion I shouted at her when she complained at the end of one season about Arsenal not winning any trophies and that all the players and the manager should be sacked. I advised that maybe if she supported a football team and not a Premiership multinational Corporation then she would be able to relate to the phrase 'taking the rough with the smooth'. Unfortunately, Natalie soon introduced me to the phrase 'sleeping on the couch'. Some people can be childish; I remember the time Natalie butted into a conversation I was having with someone about a local Sunday League team with "Arsenal this and Arsenal that" to which I retorted that we were discussing a football team and not a multi-national Corporation. Shortly after that I went to clean the remnants of Natalie's drink off my face.

One of Natalie's favourite mistakes was to bang on about a player and get their name, club, position or nationality wrong. I once had to explain that David Gerrard was actually Steven Gerrard who played midfield, not defender, for Liverpool, not Chelsea, and England, not America. Natalie once bleated on that Thierry Henry was a bad player because he had never played for Arsenal. One of her observations was that she felt it unfair that David Beckham played for England. I pointed out that was because David Beckham is English; Natalie insisted he was

American because he played for an American football club. Other international incidents included, "What does Cesc Fabregas have to do to get into the England team?", "People always mention Northern Ireland and the Republic of Ireland teams but never the Ireland team!", "Why aren't Argentina allowed to play in the European Championships?" and that she felt it unfair that "Korea gets two teams but Arsenal aren't allowed to play in the World Cup!" Matches live or on TV were extremely hazardous, too. I lost count of how many times I had to explain the rules such as corner kicks, throw-ins and goalkeepers' shirts; I had to explain that the ref can't go lightly on particular players because they were good-looking; yes they did have a bath after the game and didn't walk around 'all sweaty' for the rest of the week; that the players' mothers didn't mind them getting dirty because they didn't have to wash their kits; and also it's perfectly acceptable to propel the ball with your head. The end came for myself and Natalie when she wanted to know, "What happened in 1966?" followed by "Did they have the World Cup that year?" augmented by "Didn't Argentina win that one? That Madonna bloke used his hand, didn't he?" and finally completed with "England didn't win the World Cup – even I know that – I really wish people wouldn't treat me like I'm stupid!"

Katie, on the other hand, liked football and knew what she was talking about; on a number of occasions she had shut up countless big mouths who thought they knew everything, and on another occasion she questioned why Sid would sing a particular song relating to Birkenhead being wonderful with its T, F and the Rovers when only the Rovers were of any interest to him, prompting Sid to be, for once, silent.

On the final day of the season we walloped Northampton Town 6-0. Tranmere had had an amazing turnaround, from a typical slow grinding start; we got kick-started around the time I met Katie. The more my relationship with Katie progressed the better the Rovers got; it was eerie as if the two had a link, as if there was a third wheel in our relationship. But that was it, the season had finished – what do we do? Apart from a couple of meals at the Italian the only dates seemed to be at the Prenton Park or at the football.

I went to see my own personal agony aunt, Jean. "Try the Albert Dock!" she told me. "I went there with Harry when it first opened...I miss Harry..."

"I miss him, too," I said to Jean. "Not the same at Prenton anymore without him."

"It's why I don't go anymore," Jean added, "it isn't the same!"

"The Albert Dock you suggest then, Jean?" I asked.

"Yes," said Jean, "it's a bit unusual, not a place you'd normally go!"

"Normal? What is normal?" I questioned.

"Same old places, same old faces!" stated Jean. "Take your lady friend somewhere different!"

I pondered. "It's worth a try..." I said.

"Well there you go then!" said Jean. "Do you think she might be the one?"

"I do!" I said in a haze. "From the first moment I saw her at Prenton Park, I said to myself, 'that's my future wife!'"

"Will there be wedding bells?" asked Jean.

"Possibly," I replied.

"You'll be able to get up to some...you know!" said Jean, suggestively.

"Some what?" I asked dreading the response.

"You will...CONSUMMATE your relationship!" said Jean even more suggestively.

"That will be nice," I said with a cringe. "I can't wait for that!" I lied. Know that my relationship with Katie was well and truly consummated; however, is it me or is there nothing worse than a pensioner talking about carnal activity?

Actually, there was one thing worse than a pensioner talking about carnal activity and that was my annoying cousin Aubrey from Southport talking sex or as he put it so embarrassingly s-e-x. And he always said s-e-x in a loud and slow voice as if he deliberately wished to be heard. He was always an attention seeker; I've always hated them along with tennis and glory hunters. I was still living at home working for a plumbing company near Hamilton Square at the time; I was lying on my bed trying to get some rest one Saturday afternoon during the off season when I heard my youngest sister talking to her newly-found favourite cousin about this new boyfriend of hers. He was some big shot from Liverpool who had got her drunk the previous weekend and got her home for some hanky-panky and the like; not what I really wanted to know. Then it began; Aubrey began to pry into every intricate detail of the tale before asking if they had s-e-x. Not wishing to know about my younger sister's sex life I instinctively turned on the radio, very loudly. Very quickly I was told to "turn that racket off" by Aubrey because it wasn't the current soppy little flavour-of-the-month boy band that both he and my sister enjoyed so much and claimed they would never love one band as much as they did then. Well, until the next new flash in the pan came along.

Once the radio was off I belted out of the door like a young boy trying to escape cub-scout camp, heading for a sanctuary away from their conversation which was now heading in the direction of 'Don't Need to Know' but not until I had heard a certain cousin who had now turned his back on religion admit his virginity, that he preferred boys to girls and that he hadn't found any suitable young men to go to bed with and have s-e-x. How delightful, what a way to enjoy a Saturday, I thought...

Although I initially had my doubts the Albert Dock were a success. From singing *Ferry Cross The Mersey* on the Mersey Ferry in very predictable fashion, to walking around the boutiques, enjoying a bite to eat, spending some money on Katie and enjoying a good smooch to singing *Ferry Cross The Mersey* on the way back to Birkenhead. We had a great time. Jean was right; a change of location did us good, different places, different faces. We got the usual odd looks there and back on the ferry as we sang the Gerry and the Pacemakers classic but then you do don't you.

A friend of mine, Robin, once said that essentially there are two types of people in this world: good people and bad people. Regardless of the colour of your skin, your ethnicity, your religion, your sexuality, your height, your weight, your gender, your age, how much money you have or the way you put on your shoes there are just two types of people when we get down to it. As we travelled back from Liverpool on the ferry we experienced both types; cheerful people who could see we were trying to enjoy ourselves as we sang a certain Gerry and the Pacemakers song; people who realised we were no trouble. Then there were the horrid sneering people who thought that we were sad and needed to throw abuse at us; and the sour-faced misery guts who thought we needed to walk around looking serious all the time.

I once had neighbours who were sour-faced misery guts, everything I did was completely wrong. Going to the pub – wrong. Smoking – wrong. Listening to popular music – wrong. Eating food – wrong. Having a sense of humour – wrong. Breathing – wrong. Not wearing a collar and tie all day everyday – wrong. Leaving my house to go to work – wrong. Trying to earn honest money – wrong. Being a plumber – very wrong. Owning a cat – extremely wrong. These neighbours of mine believed that a young person like me should be concentrating on going to church, watch only current affairs on the TV, not smiling, be in bed by 9 o'clock and read only *The Times* and the Bible all whilst wearing a collar and tie. We had a monumental row when their horrid little yappy terrier got into my backyard and cornered Dolly; an absolutely terrified Dolly scratched the dog before I chased it off. The couple complained that my cat was dangerous and had provoked their little darling by just being in my backyard. I argued that they hadn't repaired their fence and their dog was in my garden. After a war of words and legal threats they moved. I've heard that they ended up with an ASBO for making another couple's life hell. Apparently the horrid little dog bit the dust; it went after a child on the other side of the road and was flattened as it ran across the road. Oh dear, my heart bleeds.

Jean gave us a few ideas for different dates, not just the usual going to the cinema and meals out, but some slightly strange ideas. Ness Botanical Gardens was unusual but pleasant, Knowsley Safari Park was eye opening, and on the way back from Ellesmere Port Boat Museum on a bank holiday Monday we found a great fish and chip shop in Bromborough. My favourite time with Katie was a weekend in Llangollen: we rode the steam railway, we watched the rain bounce off the trees and plants, we cuddled up for the whole length of the trip. I told Katie I wanted to spend my life with her.

Llangollen was a real spur of the moment job. I was sat at home one Monday afternoon having had no work on when my uber gorgeous girlfriend comes storming into my house. Hacked off with a day's work in the bank and ready to vent her anger on the world she stormed in ranting about her day of stupid customers, stupid colleagues, ignorant customers, ignorant colleagues, vending machines that wouldn't work, toilets that couldn't be accessed, taxi drivers who wouldn't stop, bus drivers who were rude and the fat woman with the skin problem who works in the general store near the bank. I must say Katie looks beautiful when she is angry.

I didn't get to the bottom of the issue and these were just the bullet points so once she had ranted herself to a standstill and eventually calmed down, we'd had a bit of a kiss and cuddle, something to eat and another kiss and a cuddle, I logged on to the Internet and booked a weekend in a cottage near Llangollen. I felt we needed it, just to be away from Rock Ferry for a short break and to see how we would get along with each other for a weekend. Katie was a bit shocked when I told her but was definitely up for it. I hired a car for the weekend and that Friday teatime we headed for North Wales. Being the kind of guy I am, I decided that a hire car would be best. I kind of felt that a battered plumber's van was not the ideal mode of transport when trying to enjoy a romantic weekend with the girl you wish to spend the rest of your life with. A couple of hours later we were in a charming little cottage in North Wales and I cooked my patented Chinese-style chicken and mushrooms for supper; we settled down with a movie and enjoyed a bottle of wine. Then we went to bed.

Just as we arrived at the cottage it was beginning to rain and by the time we got to bed it was raining considerably heavier. That night was a momentous night for Katie and me; as the rain hit the panes on the windows I really began to talk about the physical side of our relationship. Sex between us had always just happened because of the great natural synergy we had so we didn't really talk about it. That night I chose to, that night it was different, that night was simply amazing.

Ever since I'd started to notice myself down there I found something arousing about the rain outside whilst laid in bed. I found it even more arousing when I was in bed with a beautiful woman. Once we were cuddled up in bed I began to tell Katie about how I felt when it rained; Katie wasn't surprised when I told her; she explained that she found herself aroused too in a similar situation. We made love; it was amazing, so gentle, so passionate, and so beautiful.

Normally I'm not one to be up early in the morning when I'm off work but that weekend it was different; we were up at half past six, we had some breakfast and went for a stroll. It began to drizzle and we returned to the cottage. After lunch we rode the steam railway and I made my intentions clear to Katie; she looked so beautiful in the rain. We found a secluded spot in the woods near the cottage, I threw my jacket on the ground, Katie lay down on it, and I pulled down her denims and made love to her. With the rain beating down on my bare behind and the rain soaking into Katie's I felt so invigorated. We returned to our cottage, took off our wet clothes and made mad, passionate love in the shower. It was all so amazing.

That night as we lay in bed we had an interesting conversation. As I entered the bedroom that night Katie was lying in bed reading a book; she usually wears contact lenses but tonight she was wearing her glasses. She looked stunning in glasses. Angry and wearing her glasses she looks stunning, kind of like the naughty secretary meets the warrior princess.

I slipped the book out of her hands then I slipped under the covers. We kissed.

"You look amazing!" I told her as I gazed into her beautiful eyes. I slipped her glasses off and we kissed and caressed.

"What do you think of the name Maria?" she asked with a smile

"It's nice," I told her in between kisses.

"Good!" she replied as she returned my kisses

"Why ask?" I asked suddenly

"Well if I have a daughter I'd like to call her Maria!" she replied smiling her beautiful smile.

"You might not have a daughter," I replied. "You might have a son!"

"That's okay," Katie answered. "If I have a son I'll name him Robert after my grandad!"

"Oh, that's nice!" I replied and we began to kiss and caress once again. Suddenly I stopped like a driver hitting an emergency stop. I looked down at Katie as she gazed up wondering why I had stopped.

"What's up?" she asked.

"You're not, are you?!" I asked with alarm.

"I'm not what?" she asked innocently.

"You know... in the family way!" I stated with great trepidation.

"What if I am?" she asked.

"Well...it's...I'm...we've..." I spluttered.

"Do you have a problem if I am?" she asked with concern.

"No, but we've not been together that long..." I began, "there's still a lot more I want to do with you before we have children together..."

"You want to have children with me?" Katie asked suddenly.

"Yes..." I said, softly. Until then I'd never wanted children, parenthood had never featured on my radar but when it came to Katie it was there. "If I was going to have children with anyone it would be you!" I added. "I love you, Katie..."

Katie smiled, from the look on her face I thought she was going to cry, she looked so beautiful

"I love you, too!" she whispered.

"So are you?" I asked. "Are you pregnant?"

Katie smiled again, she shook her head. "No!" she whispered again. "I was just thinking, I would really like to have children with you...!"

Even now when I look back on that weekend I think it was the best time of my relationship with Katie. That weekend was so important; I really clarified how I felt about Katie and I really sent home how much of a commitment I was ready to make to her. I was really beginning to think that Katie was The One and I would be spending the rest of my life with her.

Those couple of months were amazing; we did so much in so little time. We never failed to have a good time. When we went out it was great. When we stayed in we had a wonderful time. When we went to bed it was mind-blowing. We had sexual synergy, we instinctively knew each other's right places and how we wished to be loved.

People thought we were the perfect couple, from the bloke on the ferry and the conductor at Llangollen, to the staff at the Prenton Park, to close friends like Jean and Sid. Both Jean and Sid thought the world of Katie; on separate occasions they both pulled me aside and told me she was The One.

CHAPTER SEVEN

In Which Love is Terminated

There's an old adage that goes something along the lines of being able to choose your friends but not your family. Katie, for some bizarre reason, had been pushing to meet my family. For reasons already mentioned I wished to keep my family at a safe distance from Katie. I could find them painfully embarrassing at the best of times; every one of them has at some point caused some kind of embarrassment to me when it came to love. It was always a concern that they would make me look foolish. History had told me that they always did. And history also told me that they always did manage to embarrass me. Countless times when I had brought a lady friend home I would walk into the living room of our family home on Highfield Road and my mother would have the family picture albums out and recall every possible embarrassing anecdote of when I was a small child. Such as the time we had a family trip to the Isle of Man and I fell into the river at a place called Cornaa. That was pure embarrassment, not just the falling in bit but it being recalled countless times ever since. My eldest sister took great pleasure in deliberately causing me to split from a girl named Anne. She would purposefully hunt us down if we were out or if Anne was alone; she would slate me to high heaven and dig as many skeletons up as possibly. She took immense pleasure in making me look stupid and foolish.

The eldest sister was at the time going through a holier-than-thou phase. She had become a hard-line atheist so she would frequently threaten people who showed any religious inclination. I'm not a religious person, I don't believe in God or go to church but that doesn't mean that other people can't. If people want to follow a religion let them as long as they don't force their opinions on me. My sister on the other hand believed people should believe what she told them, ironically telling people they shouldn't be told what to do by brainwashing religions. It didn't help that Anne's family were Catholics, and my eldest sister was dating another sociology student with a high-and-mighty attitude plus an extremely big nose: he was a teetotal, non-smoking, vegetarian atheist with an anti-American point of view who lived off what he described as his rich mummy and daddy. Those were his words; yes, he was a grown man who called his parents Mummy and Daddy. My sister quickly turned from a chain-smoking, cheeseburger guzzling, Special Brew assassin to an obnoxious vegetarian bigot; one of those people who is instantly against anyone who doesn't conform to her lifestyle and is extremely vocal and hypocritical about it. The lifestyle ultimately didn't last; the hypocrisy did though. Like the majority of my elder sister's relationships, it didn't last. In a bizarre twist the hard-line atheist found the Lord Jesus Christ whilst on holiday in America and went to live with a religious sect down in Dorset; last we heard he was now a she and went by the name of Mother Gwendolyn.

It was always a concern that the elder sister would make me look foolish and stupid but that could never be said about the youngest sister. The apple of her father's eye she was the only one she could make look foolish and stupid. Easily confused at the best of times she once stood outside an art gallery for a whole afternoon waiting for her date to appear. "He said we were going to the pictures!" she howled miserably later; her date had meant the cinema. Oh dear...I still remember the evening Sara came round. Sara, with the exception of Katie, was probably the most beautiful girl I had ever dated. Ever since that disastrous night I was forever telling myself that I should have married her. If it wasn't for my family, I told myself, I would be married right now to a really beautiful girl.

Sara was unbelievably intelligent; she was a doctor at Mossley Hill Hospital. I remember the first time I met Sara; it was at a sports centre, I had been talked into playing 5-a-side football and just as we were taking to the court a ladies' basketball team were coming off and I saw her clad in her kit. She smiled, I drooled, and I started talking to her, and somehow we ended up with a date. We dated for a few weeks and I began to think she might be The One. And then she asked to meet my family. I was instantly full of fear

My fear was justified. The evening started out badly, then slowly became awful before eventually ending up a disaster. My eldest sister, who was at the time seeing a Straight Edge advocate (a teetotal, non-smoking, drug-free preacher of abstinence who also had appalling body odour), kept coming out with comments about doctors, hospitals and medicine being unnecessary and that medical professionals were simply the manipulators of the weak, ignorant and lazy. She continually mentioned how she was an advocate of alternative medicine and her visions of a Straight Edge Utopia; I'm better than you because I'm Straight Edge, she kept telling us all. That was until my father asked her how the rash was. This was a rash that was caused by one of her alternative medicines.

Dear old Dad. He was still with us then. As a rule he seemed to be the most reliable and least embarrassing but that night the rule went out of the window. From the first moment Sara entered the family home, he was transfixed on her very lovely legs, then kept patting her on the knee, staring at them, making countless references to nurses in black stockings, and I thought he was going to have a heart attack when Sara bent over to pick something up off the floor. I half expected him to her ask if she wouldn't mind sitting on his lap.

My youngest sister made herself look like a right moron, which as you already know was nothing new. She explained how she had been to the hospital a number of times, like the occasion when she fell over drunk and the other time when she "needed a poo but couldn't have a poo" (her words, not mine), but they weren't like the hospitals you see on television. You didn't get that nice Charlie bloke they have on *Casualty* and you don't really find out which staff members are shagging who because they won't tell you. Plus, my sister added, they didn't half get cross when she lit up a cigarette in the ward, you'd have thought she had done something really wrong like share someone else's bath water. She really did know how to make herself look like a prize fool.

The meal was what could generously have been called bland; my mother as a cook likes to cook things until there is no flavour left. "Flavour is something that other people experience," my father once explained following one particularly bland dinner. Then my eldest sister began telling unfunny, sarcastic and downright offensive 'Doctor, Doctor' jokes. I won't repeat any. Then my mother thought it was a good idea if we played Trivial Pursuit. "We'll show her who's smart!" she advised us with ill-judged confidence. It was a nightmare. According to my youngest sister the famous steam engine designed by George Stephenson that won the Rainhill trials was Thomas the Tank Engine and my father incorrectly informed us whilst staring at Sara that Australian cricketer Shane Warne is an exponent of nice legs. My eldest sister refused to participate as Trivial Pursuit was unfair to people of low IQs such as me and wouldn't want to embarrass me; I'm better than you already because I'm Straight Edge she advised me, I don't need to prove it. Anyway, Sara won the Trivial Pursuit, I came second, my dad third, my mother fourth and my youngest sister in last place still disputing that the capital of Iceland is all of them because all the letters in the sign are in capitals and we even had a carrier bag that said so. AND how was she supposed to know the Titanic was a real ship that sank and not just a movie. Next thing we would be telling her that Noel Edmonds didn't really live in Crinkley Bottom and he didn't throw a House Party every week. I was wondering if it would be the right time to mention to her that Santa Claus wasn't real. I decided it would be against my better judgment as explaining to my younger sister that the tooth fairies weren't real was a bad enough experience.

"That went well..." I recall saying to my beautiful doctor soon to be ex-girlfriend when I drove her home later that disastrous evening

"No it didn't!" she barked back, angrily. "They are atrocious people!"

"I know..." I agreed, glumly. "Except my dad..."

"He was the worst!" she snapped. "I thought he was going to ask me to sit on his lap!"

"He's normally well-behaved..." I began in tame defence.

"Normally?! What's normal about that lot?" Sara asked, angrily.

"I don't know!" I replied, sadly. "Can I see you again?" I asked, hopefully.

"No! I thought you might be The One, Tommy," she shouted as she got out of the car. "I thought you were Mr Right, a nice kind-hearted hardworking man but after meeting your wretched family I realised I've never been so wrong about a person! You are one of them!" she shouted hysterically through the open car door. "I never want to see you again!!!"

Sara slammed the door and promptly stormed into the house. She was right about one thing; I never did see her again.

"You've met my family," Katie began, "I really want to meet yours!"

"You don't really!" I advised Katie strongly.

"I do! I think I'll like them!" She added, "You liked my family!"

It's true. I did like Katie's family; we had met at Katie's birthday bash and when she took me down to Port Sunlight one Sunday afternoon. Her parents were nice warm people; her siblings easy-going and laid-back. Unlike my family, they didn't have a gift for embarrassing her; there was not one tale of anybody falling in any rivers on the Isle of Man. How could I introduce the love of my life to that lot in Highfield Road? It would be pure embarrassment and could easily finish Rock Ferry's greatest love affair. In the words of Jilted John it would be the end for me and you and I would be crying all the way to the chip shop.

"Well at least let me meet some of your friends!" Katie said after I wangled my way out of another girlfriend-family showdown. That was a compromise. Why not? My friends were alright. Yes she could meet them.

Through years of avoiding bullies and being called Monkey Face I managed to gain a good set of friends. In fact the one openly redeeming thing about school was the group of friends I made; some I had lost touch with: one guy is down in London running a sex line to help pay his rent whilst another is down in an RAF base in the West Country and another one of our group has simply vanished!

The first of my friends she met was Gareth; my battered plumber's van was in the need of a bit of repair and when it came to repairs Gareth was your man. Gareth spent the majority of his time tinkering with motors and anything mechanical so when he was given the chance to take over his grandfather's garage business it was a natural move. My first memory of Gareth was his eternally runny nose; he seemed to have just one friend who also had a runny nose, with whom he was thick as thieves. When his friend left our school, Gareth was a bit lost and eventually the odd little lad with the runny nose and a talent for mental arithmetic was initiated into our group. I took Katie along to Gareth's workshop where we had a brew and a chat. Nice but odd were the words Katie used to describe Gareth.

My longest-standing friend is Jimmy; to this day I'll never know how we became friends but we just did. My family just used to refer to him as your funny little friend; even when we were teenagers he was still dubbed my funny little friend.

Everyone seemed to refer to him as a bit strange, the type of person who once he had reached adulthood would most likely stack shelves in a supermarket or collect glasses in a nightclub as a profession, and as a pastime he would stand on the edge of street corners shouting obscenities. We were all very shocked when he got a job with an insurance company; we're all still shocked that he has been able to hold the job down and is now assistant manager.

I don't know how I managed it but all my friends seemed to be a bit odd or strange and a good target for bullies, namely Ricky Fatlips. On the one occasion we took pity on Ricky and he was allowed to hang around with our group, he was so unpleasant we just said no in the future. Unfortunately Ricky Fatlips couldn't accept this and began pushing us around even more. Chris took offence to this and the playground fight between Chris and Ricky was a thing of legend; a couple of punches and a kick left Ricky sprawling on the deck trying not to cry. The time Chris threw Ricky into the girls' toilet was priceless; Ricky had opted to pick on one of the infants and Chris took exception. One minute Ricky is threatening a petrified little kid, next thing he's being shoved face first through the door of the girls' toilet; a few screams from the girls later and Ricky emerged in tears. Happy days for all concerned, well maybe not for Ricky. Chris was arguably the toughest and most sensible of our group; I had started school the same day as Chris so that was where our friendship began.

I always recalled that the bullies liked to target new kids so when a lad from Dundee joined our school he was a sitting target, straight away the bullies would set in. The taunting, the threats, the stealing, the blackmail and when the big ugly thug with the peculiar-shaped head two years older than us who liked to use shoes as footballs chased after him, we stepped in. So we befriended him and came to know him as Haggis.

I always remember when we 7 or 8 and Jacko told everyone

about his hobby – Airfix kits. He beamed with great enthusiasm, his chest puffed out, as he told us about what he had put together, his favourite kit and what he would really like next. As a friend he was easiest to buy a birthday gift for. Any Airfix kit you could lay your hands on. He is now the manager of a model shop. Once a nerd always a nerd I suppose.

Our group stuck together all the way through infant and junior school and the last of our group joined in the final year of junior school. Rossi was a lad from a very poor part of Wallasey. He had a very sad background; after his mother was arrested for working as a prostitute he had been sent to live with his aunt in Rock Ferry. An instant target for bullies, we initiated him into our group straight away. Sometimes I felt like my friends and I were chosen rejects; the group of misfits who banded together as we didn't think we would fit in with anyone else.

Eventually the big night came; my friends would meet the lovely Katie who I had told them so much about. The pub near the Rock Ferry station was the concluded venue. Why? So we could go into the pub and annoy the natives in there. One thing they didn't like was non-local natives setting up camp in their pub; they hated the quietness of their bar being broken by people who, they believed, didn't know their place and didn't want to sit in a room reminiscent of a doctor's waiting room. If we were going to have a good night we'd annoy that lot, we had to make them aware that not everyone wanted to sit in an environment reminiscent of a doctor's waiting room.

We had a great night. Katie got along with everyone fantastically; Rossi brought his girlfriend along and Gareth brought his wife. Jacko brought along a fat woman he was trying to get 'jiggy' with and Chris' brother came along for a good crack. About 11 p.m. an enforced last orders was called by the miserable landlord and it was time to move on. Chris suggested a nightclub; I declined and so did Katie. Chris said they were going to a club in Clifton Park. I whispered quietly to Chris that I didn't feel that particular place would be such a good idea. After I reminded him of my stomach he agreed.

It was a beautiful summer night; the sunset over the Mersey earlier that night had been fantastic. I walked slowly hand in hand with Katie to my home.

"What did you think of them?" I asked Katie.

"Nice," she told me, "bit odd and a bit strange but nice!"

"Good," I added, "it's good you like them!"

"That pub is weird," Katie began.

"It always has been!" I told her. "What shall we do now? It's been a great night so far..."

"Sex?" said Katie, suggestively.

"What about it?" I asked.

"It's where two people bounce around together in bed," Katie advised.

"Oh that's what they call it, that thing we do..." I replied.

"Do you fancy some?" Katie asked.

"Why not?" I replied. Good night had by all, I thought.

During those magical few months I knew that Katie was the one for me. Sid suggested I have a day out at New Brighton with Katie. He had said he'd been there with one of his special friends and had a great time, so we followed on from Sid's advice of going and went. We'd gone to the bowling alley, enjoyed the amusement arcade, walked to the Fort Perch Rock and had some ice cream on the front. As we walked along the front I told Katie I thought it was time that we moved on to the next level. It was on the front at New Brighton that I asked her to move in with me. She smiled that beautiful smile of hers and said, "Yes!" It was like music to my ears. But she had a question for me. "Those scars on your abdomen; what happened to you?" she asked.

"I was involved in an incident a few years ago," I told her. "Very unpleasant, I don't like to talk about it!"

I thought that would be the end of the matter; why am I oh so wrong about these things?

I would tell Katie about the bottling in my own time; it would be a hard subject to deal with straight away. It would involve delving into one of the darkest chapters of my life which I wasn't ready to revisit. However, one thing I never told Katie the moment she agreed to move in with me on that glorious day in New Brighton was that I had begun to plan our wedding. She was The One and if we made it to six months I would pop the question.

I couldn't decide on church or registry office, large scale or small scale, home or away. I didn't want to tell her unless she thought I was unmanly. She viewed me as a real man and she always said to me she liked men to be men. I must admit I got a bit self-conscious about it. I became concerned about what I ate, how I dressed and what I watched on TV. Trying to get through *Titanic* without shedding a tear or an unmanly look on your face is extremely difficult; drinking wine with a meal can be hazardous and please don't talk to me about buying clothes! Then there was the ordeal of proposing marriage to the woman I loved; how would I go about that in manly fashion? You have to remember that there is a stigma about flowers being for wimps, the down on one knee was a bit clichéd and singing was out of the question in case, despite my fantastic voice, I chose anything too soppy. I always remember some soppy little fool going on *Stars in Their Eyes* as a soppy boy band member and crying when he went through to the final. There was nothing particularly manly about that at all.

I had only proposed to one person in my whole life; her name was Sarah, not to be confused with my former doctor girlfriend Sara. Sarah was a punk who happened to frequent a couple of places I liked to go myself. We got along quite well as friends in general so it didn't come as a shock when we ended up in the same bed one evening. It was after the festivities had concluded for the evening and we had mutually agreed a good sleep was in order when I popped the question for reasons unknown. Sarah said she was very flattered but she didn't think her boyfriend would be too impressed if she got engaged to somebody else. Oh dear...

The last weekend in August was set to be the day she moved in. I bought our season tickets for the new season and the future looked so bright. We found even more common ground. We both liked cricket. It surprising because a lot people believe that watching cricket, yet alone enjoying it, should be a crime. At Jean's recommendation we watched a Lancashire game at Liverpool. I don't know what surprised me more, going to the game in the first place or going with the girl of my dreams.

Spending money is one of those things, you have to do it out of necessity in order to get the basic things in life, should it be food, water, shelter and warmth, or you spend money because you want to. With Katie I did it because I wanted to. I didn't mind spending money on Katie because I loved her, but it did bother her, I could tell. That's me spending money on her and not that I loved her. I just like to clarify that point! Katie always tried to pay her way but I just couldn't let her. Hey, I was in love.

Katie is not one of those women who take the mick when it comes to money. A lot of women will date a man at the expense of their pride and reputation simply because the man has a lot of money. Some are greedy, some are foolish, and some are both. Katie was neither; regularly we split the bills at restaurants and she always bought her share of the drinks when she could. I've known women who just take, take, and take.

I'm always a bit nervy of letting women know I have money, it's how you get the attention of the unwanted. The previous summer I gained an admirer from hell (yet another horror bag), a sad, fat psycho who looked like she had a spare tyre around her waist. She took a shine to me for some bizarre reason; most likely because she was not right in the head and I have this remarkable ability to attract nutcases. She was even more delighted when she heard I had money from my own business. The horror bag in question had three children, from a previous relationship to a waste of space, to whom I would be adjusted and accordingly then learn to accept them as my own before we planned our future together; well that's what she told me. At this point I was really freaked out; I'd known her less than an hour and she had our future planned. Then my horrific admirer advised that it was a good thing I had money because I would be able to support her children and she would be able to concentrate on spending her benefit money on weed. Or maybe I would like to buy the weed for her and she could keep the benefit money for other things. I ran a mile to get away from her at the next convenient opportunity.

Being in love can make you act bizarrely. One job I did for this lady, I let her have it for free because she was a nice lady and I was in love. I tipped a waiter 20 quid just because I was in love. But the course of true love never runs smoothly...

Love has never run smoothly for me; from those very first crushes to the doomed relationships with the Hannahs and Natalies of this world, it has never gone right. Finding out that a gorgeous blonde used to fancy you rotten when you fancied her rotten, too, a few years earlier but you didn't say anything is a shot to the solar plexus. Especially now that the said blonde is now married and I can only think of what could have been!

I also had a bizarre night where I finally managed to have a smooch with a woman I had fancied for absolutely ages. I walked her home and she invited me in, but then decided that she couldn't go through with anything because there were children in the house. Fair enough, I thought. She escorted me to the door where we smooched again outside and just before I could ask her out the front door ripped open and her fuming husband stood there. He jabbed me twice on the left cheek whilst I tried to explain I had made an innocent but foolish mistake and was not aware that she was married. After he had advised his wife that she would be packing her bags in the morning, he turned his attention to me and still not listening to my comments that I had made an innocent and, yet foolish mistake, he took a swing at me, still refusing to listen to my point. He eventually saw my point when he got acquainted with the pavement courtesy of my left fist.

Ever had one of those evenings when you spend the night talking about the woman you are in love with to another woman then finding out you could have had a little action with said woman if you hadn't talked about another woman? I've had a few of those. Well, if that makes any sense at all. I digress.

There are many ways that love may end abruptly; the usual way is when boy meets girl, boy tells girl he really likes her and girl tells him that although she is very flattered boy is not her kind or girl tells boy that she doesn't have time for anybody, only to start dating someone else two weeks later leaving boy hacked off.

Other ways involve boy coming home from a hard day's work to find girl in bed with another boy resulting in the first boy breaking the second boy's nose and the girl being sent off to live elsewhere. Or even boy coming home to find girl has run off with half the contents of boy's house which is particularly painful and costly indeed. Much simpler ways of terminating love abruptly are girl not turning up at the cinema for a date or boy blowing all his wages for the week just for a cuddle and a peck on the cheek where he realises that the girl is completely and utterly not worth it. The more complicated ways for love to end have included girl summoning boy for a serious chat about their relationship that results in girl telling boy that after sleeping with him that she is now one hundred and ten per cent sure that she is in fact a lesbian and will be moving in with another woman who lives in Storeton next Tuesday. And then there are the downright ridiculous manners that the path of love is cancelled.

Picture this, it's a nice summer evening the second week into

June and boy plus very attractive, interesting and intelligent girl are walking along Bebington Road past Victoria Park in the direction of a nice cosy little restaurant for a nice cosy little meal and hopefully back to her place for a nice cosy little bit of 'how's your father'. A nice red car is driving along the road in the direction of Bebington or Storeton when three grotty pigeons strut across the road. As timing has it the last of the pigeons manages to strut right under the wheel of the pretty red car resulting in a loud pop and a cloud of feathers.

Humoured by the pop, boy begins to laugh at the pigeon's unfortunate demise causing the horrified girl to tear into her insensitive date, first verbally then with a handbag. As boy tries to apologise and explain it is merely a 'disease-filled and spreading pigeon' girl continues tirade much to the humour of many a passer-by who like the shopkeeper from *Mr Benn* and fair-weather football fans have suddenly emerged as if from nowhere. Eventually, girl flags down passing taxi before informing extremely embarrassed boy that she never wants to see him again because he laughed at the misfortune of the poor deceased and extremely flat pigeon just as boy's long-time family friend has walked round the corner and witnessed the whole inglorious incident.

I still can't mention pigeons now without Sid going off on one about the whole ex-pigeon incident. Never mind, eh? It was only a pigeon, wasn't it?

The Rovers had got off to a flyer in their first season back in English football's second tier for a number of years. Three games played, three wins, six goals for, one against, nine points. We had gone to the first two home games, Blackpool and Scunthorpe our respective victims. Suddenly I had it all. My own business, my own home, my club was flying high and I had a gorgeous girlfriend who was about to move in me. However, my old friend fate would throw a spanner into the works.

It was the week Katie was supposed to move in. I was in my

kitchen one evening in late August doing the washing up and Dolly was playing with a piece of string when Katie let herself in. I noticed she was strangely quiet and there was clearly something bothering her. She poured herself a glass of orange juice then broke her silence. "I saw Jordan today," she said, coldly.

"Did you? I bet that was unpleasant!" I replied. Who cares about that tosser, I thought. "What did that waste of space want?" I enquired.

"He told me about those scars on your abdomen," she began. I paused nervously as I did the washing up, I didn't like the sound of her voice. "How could you?" she asked, her voice shaking.

"How could I what?" I asked with trepidation.

"You fractured his ribs and punctured his lungs!" she shouted. "No wonder he bottled you!"

"Yes!" I quivered. "He bottled me!"

"Because you beat him up!" she replied angrily.

"No, he bottled me then I took my revenge!" I retaliated.

"I thought you were so kind!" she said, sadly, the hurt in her voice ringing out. "He's a goddamn human being!"

"He attacked me for no reason," I tried to explain.

"He told me you beat him up then threatened him again so that is why he bottled you; he was petrified!" she cried.

"It didn't happen like that..." I began.

"He told me you would say that..." she said sadly, not wishing to believe what had happened.

"And you believe him?!" I asked angrily.

Katie looked sad, hurt and betrayed. "Yes..." she said, a tear coming to her eye.

"So you'd sooner believe him than me?" I said tearfully. "That thug, who cheated on you, stole from you then beat and humiliated you!"

"Well maybe if you hadn't destroyed him, he could and

would have turned out to be a better person!" Katie raged.

"He's scum!" I shouted. "He was scum then, he's scum now, he got what he deserved!"

Katie looked angered, "You couldn't be honest with me! I wanted no secrets between us; you didn't tell me the truth!"

"How could I?! Your ex bottled me, how could I tell you that?! How could I say you know your darling scumbag ex? He tried to kill me, you know! I love you, Katie!" I shouted.

"I thought I loved you...but I was wrong!" she cried, her voice broken by emotion. "Not after this! He is a goddamn human being and you destroyed him!"

Katie exited and slammed the door. I stood for about ten minutes laughing nervously trying to tell myself it would be okay and that it hadn't really happened, it was just my imagination or I would suddenly wake up in bed cuddled up with Katie. I resisted the chance to phone, text or e-mail. It was just a row, that's all.

When I finally got a text the next day from Katie saying it was over my world imploded; the message said that if I couldn't be honest with her then who could I be honest with. I wept for two hours solid on Jean's shoulder. I couldn't believe it, one row and it was over. One row about that thug; I couldn't believe that she had ended it all. From there everything seemed to go wrong. Work dried up, I became ill and Tranmere went downhill. It rained solidly throughout September and I caught the flu. I became depressed and not even Dolly's cold wet nose and bushy whiskers could cheer me up. I'd lost that loving feeling. Birkenhead and Rock Ferry's greatest love affair appeared to be over...

I can never decide whether fast food should really be classed as food or food poisoning. I was stood there in downtown Birkenhead one freezing cold Wednesday afternoon in late September with the raining was hammering down on me holding my tool bag in one hand and wondering whether I should go into a well-known fast food outlet for a bit of shelter and a bite to eat. I had been welcome of a job to do in a shop of dubious nature but, hey, money is money and I always need money. Well, I don't need it; I just like it. I digress.

Would I go in or would I go home? I had a pretty heavy cold; my flu had subsided and was now just a heavy, nuisance cold that wouldn't shift. During my flu endemic I had been living off takeaways and meals from the chip shop, well, actually since my split from Katie I had been living off takeaways, convenience meals and food from the chip shop a lot. I just couldn't be bothered cooking. I used to enjoy cooking for Katie when we were together but now it seemed pointless. Like a broken pencil life without Katie seemed completely and utterly pointless.

So did I go into the fast food outlet and sell my soul by buying a grot burger and manky fries with a lukewarm cup of brown? I had to get all the way to Rock Ferry before the rush hour kicked in so I had to decide quickly. But I hated that type of fast food; as a kid I had been fascinated by it, when you saw one of the adverts on the TV or a picture of the food in the paper it looked very appetising. I really wanted to try this; everyone else did. I hated it when my friends (and enemies) would blag about having meals at these fast food outlets; I desperately wanted to try this new experience. Finally, when I was 14 I got the opportunity to try a meal from a certain fast food outlet. It was a total disappointment. I was served by a grunting Neanderthal who had been part of the spillover from the local branch of the National Front and received a manky burger with a tatty garnish and some sloppy ketchup plus a cold box of tasteless, greasy French fries and a cup of coloured iced water. So that was two quid down the toilet. You might have thought I would have learnt from my first visit to the fast food emporium I had wished to visit for so long. I didn't and I must have returned a good twenty times before I concluded I didn't like food from a certain fast food outlet all along. Never mind, eh?

As the rain drummed on to my jacket and I felt the drops running down the back of my neck, with my legs feeling increasingly colder I peered in through the window still unable to decide whether to go against my culinary principles or not. I mean, Chinese and Indian takeaway are perfectly acceptable in my opinion, by having a Chinese and/or Indian takeaway we are contributing to a multicultural society. Even a nice greasy kebab can be a pleasant if flatulent experience. Now as for the chip shop, that is part of the English people's national identity. I recall as an apprentice I would treat myself to a meal at the local chip shop; a half-pound burger bap, four sausages and large chips that would be augmented by a few slices of bread when I got home; lovely. Couldn't beat the food plus I felt I was doing something for the nation and its economy

As I continued to peer in I recognised a figure that walked up and wiped one of the tables; it was a lad from my school days we had called Roswell. We called him Roswell because he looked like the alien out of the Roswell hoax. I remember how he would bang on that he was going to be a computer technician when he left school and in a few years he would be the head of an IT department at a major multinational corporation. How he was going to leave everyone trailing in his wake behind him as he soared up the company ladder. From all accounts Roswell only ever got one thing signed off on his college course, which he spent five years on. Oh how the mighty had fallen, from future businessman of the year to a lowly table wiper working for minimum wage at a fast food outlet. It's always nice to see a loudmouth fail.

He once had the gall to tell me I would equate to nothing, despite the fact I was in higher sets than him for everything and had achieved more than him in our time at school. Apparently, I lacked *it*, I had no fashion sense and I wasn't popular enough. Then again he didn't have *it* (unless *it* was a dose of head lice); his fashion sense was likened to an oversized Mothercare outfit and had only one friend. His sole friend was a fat, slobbering sycophant of a boy who went on to become a shelf stacker at a local supermarket. Seeing Roswell's fate after he had boasted as a boy somewhat cheered me up on that wet afternoon. It was just what I needed.

In the end I didn't go against my principles and indulge in a nice dose of indigestion to go with fries. I guess it was as I stood there soaking wet in downtown Birkenhead on that wet Wednesday afternoon in late September staring on at Roswell's lowly position wiping tables that I began to think of Katie, my one true love. I recalled the day of the fifth-round Cup upset against Liverpool and our fateful kiss in the Johnny King Stand when the first goal went in. Then I thought of that first real chat I had with Katie in the Prenton Park at full time as the first minutes of many man hours were lost in Birkenhead; we had spoken of our loves and loathes and one thing we both hated was fast food from a certain couple of fast food providers. I thought to myself that if I was going to get an alleged meal from that emporium it would be in spite of Katie more than anything else. I couldn't do that. I didn't spite Katie, I loved her. I would always love her.

That evening I went home with an increasingly heavier cold from standing in the rain in downtown Birkenhead; I toasted some bread and heated up a can of cheap baked beans before I headed to bed with my heavy cold and a hot water bottle. Something bugged me though as I tried to drift off to sleep amidst the smell of vapour rubs. As I had been walking away I had seen a familiar figure wearing a uniform similar to that worn by the fast food operatives who worked in the emporium where I had been stood. The individual had opened the door, in pretty surly fashion, for a woman with a pushchair. He looked at me and I looked at him; we both scowled. As I looked back at it I'm one hundred per cent sure it was Jordan.

CHAPTER EIGHT

Bring Back That Loving Feeling

The good people at BSkyB gave the long-suffering fans of Tranmere Rovers a match on Sky Sports on the last day of September. Sid brought round a few beers, told me the latest news about her from the chemists and her with the red hair who teaches PE at the high school and what they'd been getting up to; then along with Dolly we watched in despair as a depleted Rovers line-up were battered 5-0 by Sunderland. I coughed, sneezed and sniffed my way through 90 minutes of torture. Ninety minutes of the worst football I've ever seen in my life; the Rovers had been hit by a flu bug and had to field mainly reserve players. The score was opened on 7 minutes through a horrific attempted clearance which was sliced into the Rovers' net resulting in an own goal. On 19 minutes it was 2-0 thanks to a tame goal given away from a cross that should have been cleared. Sunderland were unfortunate not to get a penalty after a late challenge, a goal was ruled out through offside and some shoddy refereeing stopped Sunderland from humiliating Tranmere; the Rovers failed to get one shot on target during the first half and the players looked completely out of their depth. On 39 minutes some dilly-dallying led to a long-range shot not being prevented which resulted in the third goal. A fourth goal was added on 50 minutes after a close tap in and it was rounded off at 80 minutes via a fine headed goal. Tranmere finally managed a tame shot on target in the 83rd minute which was comfortably held by the Sunderland goalkeeper. The final whistle was a relief, the torture had ended. I must have put away at least five hot toddies over the game; the combination of my resurgent flu, alcohol and Tranmere being battered made me feel worse. Even Dolly gave up on me and went to sleep on the chair by the kitchen table.

"When it rains it pours, eh, Tommy!" quipped Sid, chirpily.

"Belt up!" I said sharply.

"Sorry!" replied Sid, clearly offended.

"I'm sorry, Sid..." I said, sadly, "not your fault – I'm very tired..."

"Have you got a sore back, have you?" Sid asked sarcastically. "You miss Katie, don't you?" he said, rhetorically after a pause.

"Yes, I do," I confirmed. "I have a sore back and I really do miss Katie so very badly!"

"I know how you feel!" said Sid, sympathetically. "I'm not talking to Matthew..."

"Why's that?" I asked.

"I called United a bunch of poofs!" Sid explained.

"We've all seen the graffiti on the back of toilet doors," I replied. "There could be an element of truth in that! And you do know about those sorts of things!"

"Plus telling him I was fed up of hearing about Nick Faldo didn't help," continued Sid. "And Wimbledon fortnight! Don't talk to me about flipping Wimbledon! It was tennis this and tennis that, enough to drive you mad!"

"Sounds like someone I went to school with," I mentioned after pondering for a moment. "Always had a few suspicions about him...you know, bit of a crafty butcher... "

"I saw Katie yesterday..." said Sid after a pause

"Did you?" I replied trying to feign disinterest.

"She asked about you, she seemed sad." He added, "She regrets that row you had."

"Did she?" I replied with a heavy heart.

"She says she wants to see you!" Sid continued.

Suddenly I felt a growing warmness inside. I didn't realise, but that loving feeling was coming back.

Sid brokered the meeting I had with Katie a week later. Katie came around to my house. We sat at the kitchen table and after some initial tension we began to talk. About Tranmere Rovers mainly; the great start; how we fell apart; the Sunderland game; how better things were under Johnny King, then discussed what Sid had shared with us both about her from the chemists and what her with the red hair that teaches PE at the high school had been getting up to. Apparently, her that teaches PE once had a thing with her that I used to go out with who moved to Storeton to live with another woman. I had also gone to school with her with the red hair and I had heard the odd rumour kicking around about her and her sexual preferences. I digress. Dolly, meanwhile, had decided to come and sit on the table between us in order to mediate and try to make sure that she was centre of attention.

"Dolly looks like she's lost weight," said Katie as she ran her fingers over Dolly's soft fur. She had leapt up on the table when Katie had arrived.

"She's missed you a lot!" I explained as Dolly headbutted Katie gently and playfully.

"I've missed her, too!" admitted Katie.

"And I've missed you – I'm sorry we had that row," I said, eventually, "so foolish...so complicated though..."

"I'm sorry, too..." she said sadly.

"Here, I've got something," I got up and walked over to the sideboard picked something up and returned to the table. "It's your season ticket," I told her. "We can go to games again!" I added.

"That'll be great!" she replied smiling that beautiful smile I'd missed so much.

"Maybe we can put this behind us and we can get back together!" I said optimistically.

Katie's smile turned to a look of sadness. "No," she replied.

"Why can't we? Not because of that row?" I asked. "You must understand that bottling incident was extremely hard for me to talk about."

Katie paused. The pause felt like a lifetime; the response felt horrendous

"I'm back with Jordan...!" she told me. "He's been a real support during our split and since I finished with him he's turned over a new leaf, he's staying out of trouble and has got himself a job in a fancy restaurant!"

I felt horrendous; I felt a twisting, tightening, burning pain in my guts and pain so severe I'd only felt it once before. It was so severe I thought I would black out. I sucked in the pain and put on a brave face. I doubt if a fireball had exploded in my stomach it would have hurt so much.

"Well, if you think that's the right decision then I hope you're happy," I told her strongly. "As long as you are happy that's all I care about!"

"That's so kind!" she whispered, but by the look in her eyes I knew she was conflicted. She didn't know if she had made the right decision. She didn't know why she had gone back to Jordan. Maybe she had gone back to him because she wanted to or maybe to spite me. But I could tell she was like me, she didn't spite me. She still loved me

Later I lay in bed; the pain had eventually subsided. Getting to bed was terrible; after Katie had left I had dragged myself up the stairs one by one, the pain hurt so much I couldn't stand. My burst appendix had never been this bad. I hoped it wasn't serious; my last trip to hospital had been a horrific experience and I wished to never have to go back again. Dolly lay beside me, she purred as I rubbed her around the ears. I was hurting, I couldn't believe Katie had gone back to Jordan; after all he had done to her, after what he had done to me. I just couldn't understand the stranglehold he had over her. He had duped her. Katie had mentioned how he had been around to her straight away when Katie had told him she had split from me. He had been able to relate to her how he had been able to change because of her and cheating on her was the biggest mistake of his life. It just seemed to me that she was being led on again by that creep recycling the same rubbish and I knew he was not being honest with her in the slightest – fancy restaurant my ass! He had struck whilst the iron was hot and driven a wedge in. What could she possibly see in that waste of human flesh and matter? I rubbed my stomach as I tried to ease the pain that still lingered. It had brought back a truly terrible memory. That excruciating pain I had felt when Katie told me she was back with Jordan, I'd only felt that once before. It had been that fateful night in Clifton Park.

At the end of an average night out I was stood outside a nightclub waiting to get a taxi home to Rock Ferry. Oh, if I'd stayed in Rock Ferry! If I'd stayed in Rock Ferry, instead of saying, "Yes, let's go to a nightclub", things would have been different. If I'd stayed in Rock Ferry I would probably have been cuddled up to Katie that very night none the wiser to who Jordan was but no, I let myself get dragged to Clifton Park when I shouldn't have left Rock Ferry, where it would be either good or bad and not average. It was a Friday night and I met up with my friends at that pub by the Rock Ferry station just because we knew, as usual, it would annoy the natives in that very pub; we had had a few drinks and around half past ten Chris suggested we head up to the clubs in Clifton Park. We all finally agreed and one taxi ride later we were in a nightclub. Slowly they started to fall: Jacko said he had work in the morning; Jimmy got knocked back at a club for being too drunk; Rossi got a phone call from his bird telling him to come home or there would be no home to come home to; Haggis pulled a girl, not a very nice girl at that, the type who are classed between plain and horror bag, are extremely shallow and think they are attractive because they're a slapper who will sleep with anything but mainly sleep with tossers; and then Chris fell asleep on the toilet before being assisted out of the club. They had all filtered away and I was the last man standing. It was familiar situation, I was always the last standing: at the time I didn't work Saturdays; I had no girlfriend and was self-employed with only a cat to answer to. I could afford it and would get the least backlash.

I remained in the last club we visited, the lager was warm and the music annoying; the toilet floor had more water on it than there was in the toilet bowls. I met a big, beautiful, cuddly girl who gave me her phone number. I was going to phone her the following lunchtime and possibly get to know her lips even better than I had already that night. Eventually, I had enough of the club. After pulling my feet across the sticky and tacky liquid-covered floor I went wading across the floor of the gents and had a final piss before I headed out of the door.

The air was fresh; it felt good against my face. I strolled to the nearest taxi rank, I had done this before, I knew the score; a few minutes later and I'd be in the back of a taxi on my way back to my nice warm bed in Rock Ferry. I'd wait for the next taxi, I'd pay five quid and I'd be home. I wondered who the driver would be – the big Geordie lad, the Rovers fan who worked 80 hours a week, the old boy who drove part-time to supplement his pension or the kind-natured blonde-haired lady who also worked the base. There was nothing to worry about or there shouldn't have been anything to worry about.

So there I was stood there at the taxi rank, just a stone's throw from the nightclub I had just left; some of the last dregs of humanity were hovering by the door, some trying to blag their way in, some trying to blag their way out. As I stood there I heard a commotion, some moron being kicked out of the club. I ignored it; the bouncers were doing their jobs. It's a job I could never have done, the obnoxious arseholes, the drunken thugs who can never accept they've had too much to drink and those individuals who insist they haven't done anything wrong; I doubt I would have the temperament. This moron insisted he hadn't done anything wrong, he had Aaron Noonan complex for sure and was constantly insisting he wasn't drunk and had done nothing wrong. The moron wouldn't go; he walked up and down the road trying to catch a taxi. No one would touch him; he kept walking into the road and the taxis would simply just drive on; when they see a nuisance they avoid them and drive on. Because of him no taxis would stop, because of him being there it all happened. If there had been a taxi there I would have got out of Clifton Park no problem, but they didn't stop because they didn't want a drunken lout in their cab. I was stood by a post, I looked up and down the road. No taxis. Suddenly I was aware of an unwelcome presence.

"What are you staring at?!" demanded a snarling voice.

"Nothing," I replied. "I'm waiting for a taxi."

"You're staring at me!" raged the voice. "Don't disrespect me!"

"I'm not, I just want to get a taxi and go home!" I assured the voice.

"Going near Rock Ferry?" the voice asked, its tone suddenly calmer.

I turned to the voice and my eyes met contact with the person later introduced to me as Jordan. "I'm afraid not," I lied. "I'm off to Wallasey," I added. I wanted to be far away from this individual, I sensed he was trouble.

"Fair enough," said the voice, "got a spare ciggie?"

"Yes," I replied. I took a cigarette packet out of my pocket and offered him a smoke.

"Got one for later?" it asked.

"Crack on!" I laughed offering another.

He lit up one of the cigarettes and staggered away; he had gone so I relaxed. My guard was down, it probably knew that, that was my fatal mistake; your common or garden thug has a sixth sense for things like this. They know when your guard is down, that's when they know how and when to strike. Suddenly there was shouting, raging and swearing; I turned to my right and as if in slow motion I saw Jordan clutching a bottle, foaming at the mouth, his face full of anger, his eyes wild, crazed, as if he was possessed. He rammed the bottle into my stomach; I remember his foul breath as he laughed a hideous, demented sound while he twisted the bottle viciously, the cracking and snapping of the glass as he drove it into my abdomen.

I dropped to the deck as the pain surged through my body, I struggled to breathe, and I tried to remain conscious. My life flashed before my eyes; my friends, my family, Dolly, Tranmere Rovers. As I began to lose consciousness I could hear him shouting, swearing, and taunting me as I lay defenceless. The last thing I recall was looking up at his face, the look of pride and intimidation on his face as I could hear him boasting, three people tackled him and then I was out. Next thing I was coming around in intensive care with my family around me and a drip attached to my arm.

I remember the time I spent in hospital; the pain and the discomfort; the worry and panic of my business, home and cat being taken away; the humiliation of coming off worse for the first time in a long while. After undergoing emergency surgery I was later rushed back in to have more glass removed; I spent my time in constant agony. The food was horrible; there was a fat aggressive nurse to whom all the patients were a nuisance. I remember the man in the bed opposite me. A pathetic old alcoholic; he stank to high heaven, he would head off to the smoking room all day before returning for his revolting meal. In the evenings he would stare at me; he asked what had happened, I told him. He told me people like me were a disgrace, people like me should not be allowed to drink, he screamed at me about his liver problems and how people like me were to blame, he wasn't allowed to drink so why should I? I had been the victim of an unprovoked violent attack but to him I had brought it on myself, even when I tried to point out I was a victim and he had brought his health problems on himself he would throw it back in my face. I remember those horrid yellow eyes and his rotting teeth; when he ate he chewed with his mouth open; he defecated on his bed five times; he urinated in his bed every night; he would shout out across the ward that if he paid tax he would be disgusted that his money was paid for the likes of me. The smell of him made me feel even worse, at times the fat nurse accused me of being responsible for his odours; in between the pain, the suffering and that revolting man I began to plot my revenge against Jordan. He was going to suffer; he wasn't going to spend a few months being mollycoddled at the taxpayer's expense, Sky TV in his cell, a PlayStation, counselling, assorted PC rubbish that fails to break the cycle of offending and act as a deterrent; he would suffer just like I had. That's why I did it.

That's why I beat him to a pulp. I didn't press charges, but I was called as witness for the public order offences he had committed; I got a good look at him in Clifton Park, I got a good look at the trial, and I knew who he was, his sentence was suspended. I had to listen to the usual bollocks about him having a poor upbringing and a sad life but he was now trying to reform his life, he had turned over a new leaf and found God. I wondered how many times his defence lawyers had repeated that garbage over the years for various lowlifes and other assorted waste of spaces. I wonder sometimes how greedy, rubbish-spewing, spineless lawyers can sleep at night with the amount of rubbish they get away with.

It was a cold winter evening when I struck; I waited for the dust to settle before I did it, I made sure it was him. I overheard him boasting in a pub about the bottling, from all the details he gave away I knew it was me he was bragging about, but then again should there be a chance I was wrong and it wasn't me I had done another poor sod a favour because if he had done it once he would do it again. I found where he drank, when he was there and why he would be there. It was a cold close night as I made my way to his haunt; he didn't notice me tucked in the corner of the pub nursing a drink as I waited to strike. He didn't notice as he left that night that I followed him at a distance, he turned into a backstreet and I called out, "Oi, Dickhead!!!" – I remember that look on his face when he turned around, that look of surprise and sudden dramatic realisation; I was the last person he expected to see. The look on his face as I pummelled him was one of terror, shock and fear. At one point I felt sorry for him but then I remembered what he had done to me and I struck him even harder. I phoned the police and took my punishment like a man.

I did nine months as a result: I pleaded guilty, and my defence put forward the circumstances. I went to prison and did my time. Somehow my business survived. Jordan is not a popular person; there were a lot of people who said he had it coming, there were a lot of people who made sure I stayed in business. Couldn't happen to a better person, I would be told over and over. Drug-dealing scum, others would say. Of all the people who spoke to me about him not one of them had one nice word to say about him. They all seemed to understand why I did what I did it. Am I proud? No. Do I feel shame? Yes. Do I regret it? No.

CHAPTER NINE

A Vitally Important Conclusion is Made

Some things in Rock Ferry never change. As I headed to the Saturday's game a man stopped me; his wife had accidently locked him out of his house whilst he was in the pub getting drunk and couldn't get in. After making a few derogatory comments about his betrothed he said he had no tobacco-based products so as a result he had to ask me for a cigarette. And, if it was possible, that he may have a spare cigarette for later.

West Brom, meanwhile, were flying high at the top of the Championship with a 100% unbeaten record. Tranmere after a bright start had now plummeted towards the bottom and there was an ominous gloom amongst the ranks of the Super White Army. The feeling before the game was one of impending defeat. It was as if everyone was wondering how badly we would get stuffed by, and pre-match there was not one murmur of a Tranmere victory. Only a few days before the Rovers were pounded 5-1 in the League Cup by the mighty Aldershot. The Shots had scored with the first shot of the game in the first minute and from then on the Super White Army went into Lance Corporal Jones mode, limbs flailing dramatically and telling everyone not to panic whilst they were the only ones truly in a panic mode; a defence that panicked when the ball went in their general direction and a goalkeeper who would have made a good window frame. At least three of the Aldershot goals could have been avoided; one of those was the second, an embarrassing own goal where one Tranmere player tried to clear the ball and it ricocheted off another Tranmere player's groin area then into the back of the net. Another goal that shouldn't have been was when the Tranmere keeper dropped the ball at the feet of an Aldershot player which resulted in a tap in. Number four saw the defence fail to close down an Aldershot forward and let him walk the ball into the net. Sid set a personal best for himself by dropping a grand total of three cups of coffee. Tranmere somehow pulled one back when a fairly innocuous-looking header ended up in the net. Aldershot wrapped it up 5 minutes from time when a blundering handball from Baker conceded a penalty that was slotted home. The Rovers were out of the League Cup courtesy of a right stuffing at the hands of a team in the lower echelons of the football league, and I had to admit that Saturday afternoon at Prenton Park versus West Bromwich Albion I didn't feel particularly optimistic. That afternoon it was cold and wet, so cold and wet I even donned a hat to keep the rain off my head and if there is one thing I do not do it is hats! And in particular berets! Confidence was low that Saturday, Tranmere were in a hole and prices had gone up in the Prenton Park. What's more, an extremely unattractive woman was working behind the bar in the Prenton Park; she'd been there about a week, she had a ghastly accent, a great big huge bent nose, oversized gums and big horrible teeth. She didn't pull her weight behind the bar, couldn't pour a drink, spent most of her time on the phone and kept trying to flirt with me. Sid thought it hilarious, and I thought it was nauseating. I don't know how I manage it but somehow all the horrors seem to hunt me down, if they're sad, fat, ugly or mentally unstable they all seem to chase me. If a woman hasn't been able to weigh herself for years because the scales don't go that high then they go for me; if they could crack a mirror with their reflection at a hundred yards then they go for me; if they have absolutely no life at all they go for me; and if they speak to themselves and have a fascination for setting fire to public places they go for me. That Saturday I was feeling what could be described as pretty low. That was until ten minutes before kick-off.

Suddenly the rain began to ease and some sunlight began to shine through the clouds; not only over the ground but also in my heart. When I no longer felt the rain on my face and saw the streaks of light I felt a presence. I looked up the row of the stand and there she was: Katie, clad in her Rovers shirt and a kind smile on her face.

That game was like old times – we commentated, analysed, we had a laugh. We recalled Johnny King. West Brom were a merciless presence, superior in every asset but somehow we hung on. Every shot was blocked, the lines were cleared and somehow there was always someone there to get something behind the ball. At about 63 minutes Chris Shuker produced a rocket of a shot from about 25 yards. It swerved and then dipped then clipped the underside of the bar before bouncing into the back of the net. We were 1-0 up; West Brom threw everything at us but we held out. The ball was hammered into the Rovers goal area and somehow it stayed out of the net, the bar was hit twice and Ian Goodison made a goal-line clearance. When the final whistle went it was a massive relief; there was almost a collective sigh of relief around the ground as Tranmere had won for the first time in ages. I hugged Katie so tight, we nearly kissed. Even Sid put in a superhuman effort to keep his coffee in his hand and off the floor.

We had our usual two pints in the Prenton Park and I walked her home. After paying further Rock Ferry Tobacco Duty, I went home, I felt good. Just as my relationship with Katie started to rekindle so did Tranmere's season. Soon we were punching above our weight, we were pushing our way up the table and we were doing it by playing good football. My relationship with Katie was back to how it was before we won League One; unfortunately the main similarities were she wasn't my girlfriend and she was with Jordan.

I was comfortable but not happy. I could still feel something there. Jean told me not to give up hope; she could tell Katie still loved me. Jean said to me it will happen, just give it time. Sid said not to force it, sometimes life is like farting, don't force it or you'll end up like Windy. That was metaphorically and not literally, of course.

"I saw you elder sister last week," said Sid as he opened a packet of salted peanuts in the Prenton Park one Sunday evening.

"I bet that was fun!" I said, sarcastically.

"She's got a new boyfriend!" Sid added.

"Oh goody!" I added with heavy sarcasm. "Let me guess – an opinionated sociology student just for a change?"

"I didn't like him..." said Sid, quietly.

"Well she always knew how to pick them!" I replied, bluntly. "What was this one's major malfunction?"

"He was National Front, wasn't he!" said Sid, in an extremely uncomfortable voice. "She threw a load of abusive verbal at me, it looks like she has adapted to bigotry quite well!"

"Now that's a shock!" I murmured. My eldest sister had always been a bigot, I suppose, she always brought offensive, opinionated boyfriends home but they were inverted bigots who tried to make everyone else look like bigots when they weren't. She always made out to be very liberal but was the first to put the knife in and was always critical of others such as the mentally handicapped. "They are nice but..." she would start off before making derogative comments or her overcritical comments about those who dwelled on council estates whilst trying to make out that she was 'One of the people'. But this was a shock, I never expected her to date a National Front thug. Especially after the incident I had involving her and Dominic.

Dominic was my sister's best friend, camp as a row of tents and a professional pain in the neck. Someone so screamingly annoying you wanted to throttle them within two minutes of their company regardless of the sexuality, race, creed or class. When they were together I avoided them like the plague but one afternoon I couldn't. I was extremely irritated about something (most likely love) so they wound me up for their own enjoyment and I nearly bit. After countless words of warning Dominic began to push his luck from where I threatened to punch him before, much to my own shame. I accused him of airborne puddle avoidance; my sister went off on a rant insinuating that I had threatened him because of his sexuality. She added that I was a Nazi, I was a bigot and should be locked up and the key thrown away. After explaining that Dominic was without a shadow of a doubt the single most annoying person on the face of the planet regardless of his sexuality, I walked away. Some people really do have double standards.

"I saw Frank Spencer, too!" Sid informed me.

"They do repeat that on the TV a fair bit!" I replied, not too interested in Sid's TV viewing.

"Not the TV show!" Sid answered. "That Hannah you used to go out with!"

I groaned. "Did you?" I moaned.

"She was in that coffee shop down the Old Chester Road," Sid began. "I went in for a coffee and a bite to eat because her at the sandwich shop has put her prices up again."

"That's not very logical that, Sid," I answered, "it costs a bomb in there!"

"Well, I didn't know that at the time!" Sid advised me. "I saw Katie in there, too!"

"Yeah she works at the bank nearby," I told Sid.

"I had a little chat with Katie," Sid began. "I'm sat there having this cosy chat and telling Katie about why Daniel from Moore Avenue has been staying at a B&B recently when that Hannah storms over and starts gassing about ballet and whether I still liked it," he continued. "So to shut her up I introduced Katie."

"You introduced Katie to Hannah?" I asked uncomfortably.

"Yes," Sid replied.

"And?!" I asked speculatively.

"I said this is Hannah, Tommy's ex, and this Katie, Tommy's

other ex," Sid informed me.

"And the outcome was?" I enquired.

"Hannah started to slag you off!" Sid began.

"No shock there!" I muttered.

"Then, after a few minutes Katie came back at her listing all your pros before telling Hannah how great you are and that you are amazing!" Sid told me.

I nodded. "Good for Katie!" I said, spiritedly.

"I think it's still on," Sid added, "you and her! I think she still loves you! You'll be back together before the end of the season!"

"We'll see," I said to Sid, "we'll see!"

While Sid's comments gave me plenty to think about as well as lighting a burning beacon in my heart in hope that my relationship with Katie would be rekindled soon, I somehow managed to acquire an admirer in the meantime. It was not the horror bag in the Prenton Park, thank God! She got released from her bar job when it was found she had a problem with bank notes getting stuck to her fingers before they ended up in her pockets. Thankfully it wasn't her; my admirer was a girl working in the local paper shop. She'd been there about five months and always seemed to go dreamy-eyed whenever I would walk in for my *Daily Star*. Even when I was with Katie she went dreamy-eyed if I was to walk in. Katie picked up on it; when we went into the shop together she would start whispering about her and that she was sure this girl fancied me. I told her it was her imagination and why was it her concern because as long as I was in a relationship with Katie I wouldn't want anyone else. Problem solved. Then Sid picked up on it and this would be a completely different situation. He would continually bang on about it and when my relationship with Katie ended he kept harping on about it. Deep down I knew he meant well, he wanted me to move on but deep down even Sid knew that Katie was the only girl for me.

Sid didn't give up though, his next step was quite deliberate;

Sid goes through these phases – he shoplifts. He would never steal anything expensive or anything dangerous, just the occasional chocolate bar. Well until he nicked a Mars bar and put it in his back pocket; then sat down on it on the bus and after thinking he'd had an accident he was very relieved to find out it was a deceased Mars bar. From then on he decided to give it up. That was until about two weeks after the West Brom game.

"I get a thrill out of it!" explained Sid in an attempt to justify his actions. "This empowering buzz! A bit like watching Tranmere – could end in glory or disaster!"

"So?" I said, bluntly. "Why do you need me to come along?"

"For a distraction!" he answered with a childlike glint in his eye.

"How am I supposed to distract her?" I asked.

"Buy something," he started, "or even better you could ask her out! She fancies you!"

So there I was, as Sid was like a bug-eyed child deciding what to swipe, ordering half a pound of Cola Cubes. As she bagged the sweets for me, in a mumbled voice I asked her out. She asked me to repeat what I said more clearly and once I did I thought she was going to have a turn; she grinned madly and nodded then started giggling with excitement a bit like Muriel in *Muriel's Wedding* when she gets asked out in the video store. Sid bolted out of the door like a child caught with his hands in the biscuit tin. This girl was so enthralled I had asked her out that she didn't even notice him.

I walked out of the shop and Sid was waiting nonchalantly by the bus stop, "What did you nick then?" I asked him rather rudely.

"Nothing!" he replied somewhat flustered. "She started shrieking didn't she?!"

"Oh great!" I replied. "All that for nothing!"

"You've got a date, haven't you?" said Sid.

"Yes," I replied, "her name is Emma and we are going to that pub by the Rock Ferry station for a drink tonight!"

Sid gave me a look and with his best John Le Mesurier impression inquired, "Do you think that's wise?"

Despite Sid's concern I knew what I was doing. I purposely chose the pub down at the station in Rock Ferry because, as I have previously explained, there is nothing the natives hate more than non-regulars going in there. Well, there is one thing they hate more and that's non-regulars going in with unknown people. It's like some warped code of honour for them; they have serious issues with outsiders introducing other outsiders to something they are not supposed to be part of and to a place where they have no apparent right to be in the first place. It was like I was a protestor from one cause attempting to recruit other people to a cause they did not belong to. That place never ceases to amaze me; unless you are family of or are introduced by one of the senior natives you have to be in that pub day in, day out for two years to be even considered as being made to feel welcome. The landlord of that pub was a right misery guts; fat, sour-faced, flatulent and unkempt, he prided himself on his cask beers and his group of weird regulars.

That night it was like a doctor's surgery, I stood for ten minutes waiting to be served, the landlord explained that he had no clean glasses, so he washed about half a dozen by hand. He did this excruciatingly slowly. Then one of his kegs went so he had to change that. It's amazing, I've been drinking in pubs since I was 16 but I've never seen a keg go when nothing is being poured. I thought it might be worthwhile getting in touch with the Pope to report a miracle. The landlord just stood there drying the glasses by hand as he stared on at me; the regulars all stared on at me and then Emma. They all seemed to blink in unison. The silence was eerie and unbearable...

I must say she did look extremely lovely that night and if it wasn't Katie I had been trying to get over something might have happened. The old perverts in the bar stared at her cleavage; she sat looking self-conscious as they gawped on in silence. Two regulars got up for drinks and the landlord happily served them. Eventually he served me my drinks, once the glasses were clean. And dry. And once the kegs had been changed and after he had been as difficult as possible with the price before making sure he fobbed me off with some Jersey money in the change.

For the first part of that date we sat in silence as the regulars gawped and murmured as if we were freaks in a sideshow or a couple of people suspected of being highly wanted and dangerous criminals. Slowly we started to talk, not too loud as the natives were very interested in what we were talking about. Note to any eavesdroppers, don't send the bloke with bad breathing to eavesdrop, his breathing will give him away for sure. I think I spoke too much about Katie that night, I must have bored Emma senseless with my constant banging on about my ex and how lovely she is and all the great times we had but Emma just smiled, fluttered her eyelashes and told me how lovely I was. At the end of the night with the natives all thoroughly unimpressed with our presence I walked her home. After a bit of a cuddle and a peck on the cheek she asked me in for a drink. I declined. Emma asked me if I would like to go out again and I agreed.

The next week we went out for a meal at a vegetarian restaurant; it wasn't great food, we were both quiet and when I did talk it was about Katie. Emma just smiled, nodded and told me how Katie was a fool to let me go before fluttering her eyelashes at me. Once again I walked her home and after a cuddle and peck on the cheek I again declined her invitation for a drink.

I took her to a Tranmere game at the weekend. Emma was very enthusiastic but ultimately clueless. Katie thought it was hilarious. Every time a Tranmere player would touch the ball she would shout, "That was a good kick!" and when a player tried a weighted pass she would shout, "Kick it harder!" She gripped my arm very tightly all the way through the game to a point where I lost all feeling in it; Katie tried not to laugh as she could see I was clearly in pain. Her expression changed when Tranmere scored a goal, Emma jumped up and down almost uncontrollably before asking if Tranmere had scored, when I confirmed that they had she jumped up and down uncontrollably even more until I kissed her. Right in front of Katie. I remember the look on Katie's face; she wasn't impressed one bit, in fact I think she was jealous!

Our last and final date was at the pictures; we watched a mind-numbingly dull chick flick in a barely full cinema. Following 90-odd unbelievable boring minutes I walked her home. After a cuddle and a peck on the cheek she asked me in adding she wouldn't take no for an answer. This time I reluctantly agreed. Emma sat close and made some suggestive comments before she finally threw herself at me saying she couldn't take it anymore. She straddled herself atop of me as we kissed and groped. She peeled her top off and let me kiss and caress her firm breasts before asking for sex. Initially I agreed but once inside the bedroom, I couldn't go ahead with it; Katie was the one I wanted and Katie was the one I would be thinking of. I offered Emma my apologies as she looked on with a look of bewilderment. She asked me if I thought she wasn't pretty; I told her she was I just didn't think it would be fair to make love to her as I thought of Katie. Emma said in a very reluctant manner that she understood then thanked me for being honest, and then I left.

A few days later I e-mailed Emma to explain; I told her she was a very lovely girl and very attractive but my heart belonged to Katie and it wouldn't be until I had moved on from Katie that anything could happen. Emma e-mailed back to say she understood and she would wait as long as possible plus there would always be a shoulder to cry on and a sexy massage if I wanted one. At times I thought I might be in denial and that maybe I should go ahead and have a fling with Emma but all my feelings would surface and I knew it was Katie I wanted to be with.

It was in mid-November when I thought it was the final whistle. Following on from a one all draw with Swansea City where a Michael Ricketts side-footer had earned us the draw, Katie asked if we could forego the usual post-match drink in the Prenton Park as she had something she wanted to talk to me about. As we walked to her flat in silence I was hoping she was going to tell me she had finished with Jordan and wanted to get back together with me, but the further we walked I had a feeling it was going to be bad news. All that silence and she had said nothing, she was trying to break some bad news to me; after all we had been through I could still understand her even when she said nothing. There was still that connection between us but I expected bad news. Finally as we stood at the door she announced that she was moving to Manchester with Jordan in three weeks.

I felt that horrific, excruciating pain in my stomach I had felt when she told me she had got back with Jordan. Katie told me Jordan had been offered a job, well-paid by all accounts, a place to live, above board; it would be a fresh start for him, a genuine chance to turn over a new leaf. Apparently, he had still been out of trouble since they had split back in April. It would be a fresh start for her, too. I felt somewhat insulted, well so would you if the love of your life picked the scum of the earth over you and moved away for a fresh start; the words 'slap' and 'in-the-face' came to mind.

I rode out the pain, I wished her well, and I told her as long as she was happy that was all that mattered. Again the pain felt so severe this time I really thought I was going to pass out. She thanked me for understanding and added that she thought I was kind. But from the look in her eyes I could tell this was not what she wanted. The look in her eyes told me that the piece of dirt known as Jordan had a hold over her and she could not break it. If she didn't comply with him she would most likely be hurt both physically and mentally by him.

I walked on home to Kirkfield Grove but halfway down the road I broke down in tears. I cried uncontrollably; it was the first time I had cried since my dad died. I was on Bedford Avenue when I bumped into this old boy, he was very sympathetic and as a result he smoked half of my cigarettes and took another spare one plus a spare one for later. Once I had blubbed out my tale of heartbreak, he explained that he had recently lost his wife; well, actually he had gone to the pub got drunk and forgotten where he lived. This old bloke said he would just walk around until he remembered where he lived; he then asked me if I had another spare cig and one for later. I quickly realised that this man was a bit mad so I gave him the remainder of the packet and headed home. Sometimes Rock Ferry Tobacco Duty is justified; giving away a few cigarettes to a harmless old soul never hurt anyone. Then again cigarettes aren't supposed to be good for you, so that proved me wrong. Probably worked all his life for a low wage, I think he had earned the right for a few free smokes and the right to be a bit mad.

I didn't go to bed as it was early evening; I e-mailed Emma. I asked if the shoulder to cry on and the massage were still on offer. Half an hour later she e-mailed me a reply to say it was. Ten minutes later I was around at her place; three minutes later we were once again kissing and groping each other. A little while later we went to her bedroom and she fulfilled her promise of a massage. But that wasn't all, she satisfied me as only a woman could. We romped into the wee small hours. I could only think of Katie though; as I made love to Emma I fantasised I was with my lovely, beautiful, gorgeous Katie. I left the next morning whilst Emma was still asleep. I fully regretted that night, I felt terrible for leading her on, I felt terrible for using her, I felt terrible because I knew Katie was the one I really wished I was with.

"I didn't mean to do it!" Sid protested as I tried to clean the remnants of his coffee off my jeans in the toilets of the Johnny King Stand.

"You never do, do you!" I snapped back; at least I had a warm leg, I thought, sarcastically, to myself.

"It just slipped out of me hand!" Sid continued to protest. "It's not the first I've spilt!"

I stood and stared at Sid, "How..." I began, "how do you always manage to spill it? Every home game you spill it! Is this some kind of subconscious desire to amuse?"

"No," Sid said, uncomfortably, "I just get a bit excited like Auntie Beattie did that time in Liverpool Stadium when she belted that big American bruiser with her brolly. Have I ever told you about that?"

"Yes, you have!" I snapped, not in the mood for Sid's anecdotes.

It was a midweek game against Queens Park Rangers and Sid had expertly managed to execute his party trick. I had said nothing all game; Katie had boycotted the game because she was doing something with Jordan, and I was in a filthy mood. A series of grunts was the most accurate way to describe my conversational skills and when a Rovers player was brought down by a QPR defender minutes into the second half, Sid had got over excited and spilt his half-time beverage down my leg. It wasn't the first time he had managed this and wouldn't be the last but I had shouted and bellowed at him before storming off towards the gents. I was fuming, when it rained it poured and I was at the end of my tether. Sid had followed me in an attempt to apologise but I wasn't listening.

Sid was suddenly silent realising that the coffee had been the end of the tether. "What's up?" he asked.

"It's Katie," I told him after a difficult pause, "she's going to move to Manchester in three weeks to live with Jordan!"

"Oh my God!" said Sid with utmost disgust. "Why is she going with that tosspot?"

"I don't know," I muttered. "I just want to break his face!"

"Do not do that!" Sid warned me. "Trouble has a habit of

following you around!"

I haven't always been a bad lad. Well actually, I've never been a bad lad. Trouble and mainly bullies have had a habit of following me around when I least want it. I was a good lad growing up, I behaved, rarely got in trouble and for the majority of my adolescence I did as I was told. Plus I made sure I drank plenty of milk so I didn't end up playing for Accrington Stanley. Even when I was called Monkey Face and being pushed around by Ricky Fatlips I was well-behaved. It was when I was at the training college that I found an aggressive streak. An individual by the name of Lee McGurnigan was the person who finally dragged it from me.

All my life I seemed to have been a target for bullies; from Martin and Ricky Fatlips to the Monkey Face boys there was always someone to push me around. Lee McGurnigan was no exception; right from day one at the Wirral Metropolitan College he began to push me around. Week in, week out he challenged me for a fight on the beach at Rock Ferry; I always declined until one fateful afternoon when I was branded a coward. I was always told to walk away from conflict but there were only so many times that could be done before something inside me snapped. Every time I would walk down a corridor or enter a room the comments would begin. There's only so much a man can take of being called a sissy, a wimp and a coward; everyone has a breaking point and I had reached mine. I knew I wasn't a coward and I would prove it. Lee was the individual who sparked something dark inside me. When he told me I was dead one afternoon, I finally decided it was time to fight.

On a cold Friday evening I walked, fatefully reminiscent of a cowboy in a western picture strutting through a deserted town, for the final showdown to the beach. I remember I wore a white shirt. There was a tense atmosphere as I entered the circle of sycophants and blood-thirsty teenagers; I remember staring Lee in the eyes as he stared through me. He had turned up in

Birkenhead just as I began at the college. I didn't know how I got on his wrong side, I just had; the story of my life, I guess. Lee bragged of his days in Toxteth and why he moved to Birkenhead; apparently, he had been excluded from Liverpool for dealing drugs and being in a gang.

That evening the air felt cool on my arms inside my blood-stained shirt as I walked home with my nose blooded and my head held high. I knew the bloodied nose I had sustained was nothing in comparison to what I had done to Lee. The last thing I had seen was his battered and bruised face rising weakly off the beach before dropping back down as I walked away after my foot had made perfect connection with his jaw. Many a time he had told me how he would kick my head off if he had the chance; I thought I'd just let him know what it would be like. I must thank Lee, who now apparently runs a plastering business in London as a front for his drug-dealing empire these days, if it wasn't for him I would never have learnt to stand up to bullies. Martin would never have had to go to that Greek dentist had I not learnt from Lee. Lee taught me that every bully gets their comeuppance. We would fight twice more over the next two years and twice more I would come out on top.

Following that fateful night I became a figure to be feared, I was the man who had knocked off the drug-dealing hard case from Toxteth; I was top dog. But I was also the man to become a target; at one point every time I turned around I was being challenged for a fight. I would leave the house and I would be challenged, get on the bus and I was propositioned for a fight, go for a drink and I wouldn't get any peace, take a girl out and my night was ruined. A few I dropped, a few I walked away from, some didn't get the message and some did. The irony was that years later it emerged that Lee was a policeman's son who had been transferred to Birkenhead, he was no tough case from Toxteth at all. Even the accent he put on was completely and utterly false. He was from a very posh area down south and had been expelled from public school for smoking.

Having the image of a fighter is hard to bear at times; I never look for fights they come looking for me. I'll always stand up for the downtrodden and victimised, in a nightclub I'm like another bouncer and when provoked I'm a dangerous man.

As much as I wanted to I knew I couldn't hurt Jordan. For Katie's sake I knew I couldn't hurt him. Deep down I knew I could seriously hurt him and drive him out of Rock Ferry but I knew there would be consequences. Most likely there would be consequences for me but also for Katie. Something told me that Katie would be glad to see that back end of Jordan. But something told me he would be back with some of the biggest pieces of scum in the northwest of England in tow. I could be nothing more than a battered corpse found floating in the Mersey whilst Katie would be a battered and abused housewife verging on the brink of emotional collapse with no knight in shining armour to protect her. Perhaps she would be upset if I hurt him; she seemed to pity him at times. That night as I walked home from the match against QPR I came to a very important conclusion.

I often reflect on my bottling and there is something I've always wondered about: did Jordan know who I was? Did he deliberately go for the top dog? How did he know Lee McGurnigan? Was he put up to bottling me? Who knows? Over the years I have managed to cross a few people, mainly lowlifes and genuine scum; people who society honestly doesn't need. People like Lee McGurnigan. I have had a few run-ins with the odd drug dealer and I wouldn't be surprised if someone had put Jordan up to it.

Being top dog is, as I've said, hard. People want to knock you from your perch at any given opportunity and a lot of people who want to do that are drug dealers, pimps and other various criminals such as human traffickers and the odd hit man. They don't like the idea that a non-lowlife can be top dog. I can confirm that as an adult I've never lost a fight; I've been beaten down but I've always got back up. One night on the Old Chester Road I was jumped, two thugs came out of nowhere. They beat me down and as they backed away laughing I washed my face in a puddle before I knocked them both out.

I can also confirm I've never gone looking for a fight. Deep down I'm not violent, trouble follows me around; would it be lowlifes or fools looking to make a name for themselves, they come looking for me. Not once in my life have I struck out unless I have been threatened or provoked in a serious manner. I had a lot to reflect on that Wednesday evening; I remember my time in prison, I stayed clear of trouble and kept my head down. I got through. I had gone to prison because I had hurt Jordan, I realised it could happen again. Then again I could end up dead if I hurt him again. If I was in prison or deceased there would be no one to protect Katie; she would be alone with only Jordan to make her life miserable. I would go to her rescue if she needed it but would she want my help, would she have the courage to call out? The tempo of my life seems to change like the tempo of this tale.

After thinking about it I realised it had been over a year since I had thrown a punch. That night I made that vital important conclusion. For Katie's sake I could never throw a punch again in my life; the consequences could be fatal, not just for me but for the woman I loved. If I stood any chance of getting back with Katie I had to avoid trouble; I knew I couldn't risk being sent away either temporarily or permanently. Katie meant the world to me and as far as I was concerned she was my world.

CHAPTER TEN

The Shape of Things to Come

When Katie made her little announcement, I expected Tranmere to go into free fall. The next weekend we went down to Crystal Palace; I really expected them to batter us. I watched the game on the TV at the Prenton Park with a tremendous amount of caution. I must admit the 5-0 score line was a real shock though; the fact it was Tranmere who won 5-0 was an even bigger shock. As far as I was concerned this was an omen. You see whenever something went wrong in my personal life Tranmere would go into free fall. When my relationship with Katie ended Tranmere fell into a disastrous slump; when my turbulent relationship with Hannah was terminated the Rovers blew a play-off spot, two points from three games required and we lost all three; when my dad died Tranmere got relegated; I watched Tranmere lose to Leicester City in the 2000 League Cup final from a hospital bed after having my appendix removed; when I got bottled Tranmere went 15 games without a win. Something here was very different indeed.

It seemed that when my life was going well so were the Rovers; when I had bad news they seemed to be accompanied by things going wrong for all things Super and White. For some reason things didn't go wrong. I tried to look into it; were me and Katie supposed to be together? Was our relationship about to be rekindled? Would everything come up roses? I still loved her, did she still love me? Then again this could be the exception to the rule. Maybe this was the calm before the storm, maybe once she had left for Manchester with her delightful scumbag it would all fall apart again: Tranmere would plummet to the bottom of the table; they would be relegated just after New Year with a record amount of games left; be found guilty of an offence that breached league rules and start the next campaign with minus 50 points and from there they would eventually go bankrupt before going out of business; my plumbing business would go to the wall and I would end up losing my home; Dolly would start scratching the skirting board and when I told her off she would do a whoopsie in my beret; and when I next heard about Katie she would be eight months pregnant and unhappily married to the scum of the earth but would be too scared to leave him in case he beat her black and blue and I wouldn't be able to rescue her. Then again, I thought, that could be all a bit too far-fetched; anyway, I don't own a beret to begin with!

"I don't like her!" I said as the dart thumped into the treble-twenty bed alongside the other two.

"She's really nice! I think you and her would be great together!" Katie advised in between throws.

If you ever have to question whether or not you fancy a girl yet alone that you are in love with her then it's confirmed when you do strange things for her you wouldn't normally do under any circumstances. Okay, I'm talking nonsense – after announcing that she was moving to Manchester with an individual best described as a stain on the underwear of life, Katie in her infinite wisdom decided she would set me up with a work colleague; Katie's argument was she didn't want to see me alone. Normally I would have said no but this was Katie, I could never say no to Katie. I did my best but I just couldn't say no; she just had to smile her beautiful smile and my heart would melt. I was still feeling bad about Emma but I would do anything for Katie, so I reluctantly agreed to meet this woman along with Katie at the Prenton Park. Just meeting someone wouldn't do any harm, I thought

Her name was Kim, and as mentioned, she was a work colleague of Katie's. She was, however, completely dull and annoying. She was short and fat with a strange fashion sense augmented by a creepy voice and a warped smile. Kim wore this ridiculous scarf around her neck at all times and kept getting it caught in things such as doors, trailed into things such as pints and tangled up with things such as Sid. Sid hadn't officially been invited to the Prenton Park but turned up for a nosey parker anyway; he had once owned a Manx cat, Sid explained, and according to Sid, Manx cats are much nosier than the average house cat and as a result this had rubbed off on him. I put forward the argument that maybe Sid's nosiness rubbed off on the cat.

I digress. This woman was just plain annoying. Kim simply agreed with everything I said offering no original thoughts of her own, nor adding anything constructive to the conversation whatsoever. Eventually, I skulked off to the sanctuary of the dartboard for a bit of peace and quiet. Katie soon joined me as Kim sat and listened to Sid tell her the anecdote about her from Irvine Road with the green Ford Fiesta and what her from Irvine Road with the green Ford Fiesta had been caught doing.

"He's like an old woman at times!" I said as a dart went into the single-twenty and I could still hear Sid rabbiting on.

"That's a bit unfair!" Katie replied.

"Is it?" I said sharply as another dart went into the treble 19. "He never gives it a rest!"

"Kim really likes you!" said Katie, quickly changing the subject with an air of desperation in her voice.

"Good for her!" I said rudely as the last dart thudded into the bullseye. "I win again!" I added.

Katie looked a bit gobsmacked, "What...? How...?" she asked.

"Single-twenty plus treble-19 plus bull makes 127!" I began. "I needed 127 to win – 20, 57, 50 – I win!"

Katie looked a bit surprised, "Another game!" she demanded in a competitive woman scorned voice. "You seem to play better when you're angry for some reason," Katie told me, "you look quite sexy when you're angry, too..."

"You do that very well!" said a creepy voice that made me

jump all of a sudden. It was Kim. She stared on with a creepy smile. "Do you like darts?" she asked, creepily. "I do!"

"I play a bit and watch it on TV!" I told Kim, bluntly, trying to avoid a real conversation with her.

"He's a really good player!" added Katie. "I keep telling him to enter tournaments!"

"I never miss darts," explained Kim. "I love it!"

"Do you?" I asked curiously. "Who's your favourite player?"

"Phil 'The Plougher' Turner!" she announced in her creepy voice.

"Really?!" I replied feigning false interest realising, she was talking rot.

"I like that Barney van Raymondveld, too!" she went on further, "and that other one – Ronnie O'Sullivan!"

"That's nice!" I told her with a false smile. "Katie, can I speak to you outside?"

I led Katie gently by the arm to the door whilst Sid began to tell Kim the anecdote of why him from Moore Avenue with the limp had a visit from the police.

Once outside I told Katie straight, "There is no way I will ever go out with her!"

"But she's nice!" Katie told me. "She's a bit lonely – she hasn't had it for a while!"

I was shocked, "You want me to...?! With her?!"

"You don't have to with her," Katie informed me. "We work together and I was telling her about our former love life..."

"You told her about our former love life?!" I retorted in complete shock.

"Yes, we had great sex together!" Katie explained, unable to see my surprise. "Did you not talk to Sid about it?"

"No!" I replied, stunned she thought I routinely discussed such issues with Sid of all people. "Why would I discuss our former love life with Sid? I don't want half of Merseyside to know about our former sex life!"

"Oh! Anyway, she supports the Rovers and she can go along to games with you once I've moved!" she explained. "She's great!" Katie gave me a quirky smile. "You do look sexy when you're cross..."

"I will never go out with Kim, Katie!" I assured her. "No, never, not at all, not going to happen, I'd sooner have my internal organs removed via my arsehole!"

It was an awful date I went on with Kim at Katie's insistence. I went with Kim to a cheap, tacky little restaurant named the Laughing Sailor with no bar and a dire menu. It was dank and smelt strange. There was nothing particularly merry about it. Maybe they should have called it the Dank, Smelly Sailor. Kim said that it was her favourite restaurant and she went there all the time. Well, she was a part-time waitress there. She never had the food but was told it was very nice. On a couple of occasions or so she said.

This was not to be one of those occasions where it was remotely nice; I had some grilled rubber-like substance with a bland sauce and overcooked tasteless vegetables reminiscent of the ones my mother would cook, whilst my date had something fish-related in a foul-smelling cheese sauce. I had foregone a starter because they all seemed foul and instead watched in disgust as Kim put away a bowl of cold, bland-looking mushroom soup which had a hint of odour de feet about it, most of which ended up on her damned scarf which got trailed through all three of her courses, the washroom sink, a cup of coffee and an unknown brown liquid. Our waitress was a big, rude, fat girl to whom the patrons of the restaurant were at best complete nuisances, a total inconvenience and reminded me of the carthorse that tended to me in hospital following the unpleasantness in Clifton Park. Kim's main, well actually, only topic of conversation was her dog: where she walked it, what it ate, where it did its doings. I tried talking about the weather, current affairs and how people who talk about one subject bored me senseless but she quickly steered me back in the direction of her dog. I pointed out at one point I was a cat person and owned a cat. I was extremely stunned when Kim advised that the cat would HAVE to go when she moved in and any Chinese restaurant would be happy to have the cat and then I would be trained to like dogs. I was starting to get freaked out by this woman. I tried steering the conversation towards Tranmere Rovers and that Katie said Kim supported Tranmere. Kim pointed out that no one cared about Tranmere. Rovers and that Katie bored her senseless by talking Tranmere; "That girl is sooooo boring!" I was informed by a creepy voice. "She's sooooo dull! Did I tell you she likes cricket, too? She's sooooo sad! I hate her! I'm so glad she is going! Did I tell you what my dog had for dinner?" At that point I decided the date had concluded and I would be going home alone.

I wanted to get a taxi straight home but Kim insisted I walk her home, so all the way to her home I had to put up with more tales of interest about her wretched dog, all told with her deranged smile on her face. Kim would make references to how she hoped I would insist on coming in for coffee so I could meet her dog. The references soon deteriorated into coffee, meeting the dog and a bit of a cuddle. Soon, it was a cuddle, meeting the dog, coffee and bed. After another mind-shatteringly dull story about her dog, Kim stopped and informed me she was hoping that I would be giving her a good seeing to as she wasn't wearing any underwear, she hadn't had it in ages and how she was much better in bed than Katie was to which Jordan would testify. Following a sudden bout of nausea I quickly delivered Kim to her front door before sprinting off to find a taxi. I hadn't moved so fast since the cheap-mild incident. Katie sent me a text later asking how it went. I told her the truth and simply replied, 'Shit.' Katie replied saying that it was shame it didn't work out but her friend Libby was available. I said 'No.' Well, I tried to.

An awkward draw against Bristol City followed my disastrous date that very weekend; an early Bristol goal was cancelled out in the last ten minutes by a very dubious penalty. A Tranmere player who will remain nameless hit the deck a bit too easily and a slightly embarrassed Chris Shuker buried the ball in the net.

"It's a bit embarrassing, isn't it?" I said to Katie later in the Prenton Park.

"What's embarrassing?" she asked with bemusement, seeming a little distant.

"That Tranmere player in the match this afternoon," I told her, "the one who chucked himself on the deck to get a penalty!"

"Yeah," Katie replied, "nothing is more embarrassing than a grown man throwing himself about!" I could see she was preoccupied with someone in the pub. "Have you seen Sid?" she asked suddenly.

"I think he went to the Clipper," I began, "someone said her from the sandwich shop was in there so Sid's gone to tell her what he thinks about that tuna and sweetcorn baguette he had last Monday!"

"Oh the one that gave him food poisoning?" Katie exclaimed. "The one he's been telling all and sundry about since Wednesday in great detail?"

"That's the one!" I informed her. "The baguette that kept him quiet for a whole day!"

Katie was still preoccupied. What was she looking at?

"What are you looking at?" I asked eventually.

"That person over there!" she said.

"That woman?" I asked looking for clarification.

"I'm not sure about that!" Katie said, uncomfortably.

"What?" I asked slightly confused by her comments.

"I think that might be a man in drag!" she whispered with a grin. "I'm sure that's a wig!"

"Oh!" I said, I tried to get a good look. "No!" I said after a good look. "That's a woman!"

"It isn't!" Katie insisted. "That's why I wanted to know where

Sid is!"

"So you think Sid is an expert on these things?" I asked sticking up for my elusive buddy.

"No!" said Katie. "It's because Sid has no concept of subtlety and will ask point blank if they are a transvestite or not! Do you remember the Cardiff game and that man with the bad toupee?"

"He would, wouldn't he?" I agreed recalling the incident where he lifted the man's hairpiece off his head and we both burst into a fit of laughter. Just as we were calming down, in walked Sid setting us into another fit of laughter.

"Well that's her told!" he said venomously. "I'll never go there again!"

We both sat and grinned. "Really, Sid?" I asked.

"Yes! Worst thing I've ever eaten," Sid said firmly. "What's up with you two?"

"Katie thinks that woman is a tranny!" I told him.

"Does she?" questioned Sid.

"That person looks like they have a wig on!" Katie added, quietly.

"Excuse me, love?" Sid shouted across the room.

"Yes?" said the person timidly.

"Are you a tranny?!" Sid asked bluntly.

"I beg your pardon?" asked the person.

"Are you a bird or a bloke in drag or a bloke who has had his tackle chopped off?" Sid asked without hesitation.

"I'm a woman!" said the person in a quivering, clearly offended voice.

"There you go, Katie!" Sid said loudly. "That's a bird!"

Katie covered her face with embarrassment.

"Why did you think I was a man?" asked the woman, still clearly offended.

"She said you look like you have a wig on!" Sid advised in a loud voice.

"Well, I never!" said the woman. "That's the last time I use a hairdressers recommended by her from the sandwich shop!"

The offended person gathered her belongings and stormed out of the door. "Well that's that problem solved! Her from the sandwich shop strikes again!" grinned Sid. "The job's a good 'un!"

Katie sat in silence for a while with her face partly covered. She was obviously embarrassed by the whole incident, I mean she genuinely believed that the woman was a man dressed as a woman and had a wig on; she genuinely thought that the woman was a man. But she was wrong.

"You do have a tendency to get these things wrong don't you?" I said to her in a high-and-mighty tone.

"Which is meant to mean?" she asked, still feeling bad about the woman she had offended when she thought she was a transvestite.

"Well," I began, "you thought I'd like Kim..."

"Don't mention her! So please change the subject!" said Katie in a certain tone of voice.

"Shouldn't you be going home to that wonderful boyfriend of yours?" I asked with an element of sarcasm as I changed the subject as requested.

"No," said Katie, "he's away in London with his new boss!"

I noted no sign of disappointment in her voice that her beloved was away. "What does his boss do?" I asked with a degree of curiosity.

"He's in property," advised Katie.

"Sounds interesting," I said.

"He runs a budget travel company, too!" Katie added.

I sometimes wondered about Katie, how could such a seemingly intelligent girl be led on by a piece of dirt like Jordan? The boss was most likely the head of a crime syndicate with interests in protection and extortion and people-trafficking plus a bit of drug dealing at the weekends for pocket money. Or maybe it was just me. Maybe it was me being paranoid. Could

Jordan be capable of earning an honest crust? Had my past with him forever moulded my opinion of him?

"What happened to Jordan's restaurant job?" I asked.

"He got fired..." Katie told me.

"What happened there?" I asked.

"I'm not going to talk about it..." Katie murmured.

Oh dear it looks like he's embarrassed her again, I thought.

"Shall we make a night of it?" I asked, optimistically, hoping to change the subject once more.

"Why not?" smiled Katie with a glint in her eye.

"Great!" I added.

"Yeah, you can meet my friend, Libby; she'll be here very shortly!" Katie informed me.

Just what I needed, I thought, yet another of Katie's attempts to set me up with one of her friends. It really got me thinking; why was she doing this? Thankfully this potential set-up was over quite quickly and painlessly. Libby walked in the door, sat down, I looked at her, she at me and we both said no. Later questioned why we had both said no by Katie, I had to explain the tale of Libby and myself to her.

A few years prior when I was in-between disastrous relationships I attended a party thrown by my friend Chris where I met a charming young lady whose name I found out was Libby. We hit it off very well. So well we ended up in a bedroom for a bit of a liaison as you do at these functions whilst everyone else is in the kitchen. Following on she agreed to go on a date; a date that would end up in disaster. We tried to go to the pictures but it was closed due to a bomb scare of all things. Both agreeing a drink was in order, on the way to the bar we walked into the middle of a crime scene and had to be moved on by the coppers. Libby said never mind, I could come back to hers for a drink and things like that. But we couldn't get a taxi. And then it began to rain. We decided to walk back to Libby's and as we were walking back to hers she slipped and broke her ankle and I ended up catching a cold as I waited with her in the rain for the ambulance. Oh dear.

There are a lot of things I remember and a lot of things I don't remember. I don't remember being born, nor can I remember my first birthday; I can't remember how I became to be friends with my friend Jimmy. But there are things I do remember: I remember my first cigarette on the beach at Rock Ferry when I coughed until I vomited; I remember the first time I paid Rock Ferry Tobacco Duty to a drunken bum who could hardly stand up; I remember all those great memories of Tranmere Rovers under the tutelage of my hero Johnny King; I remember the first time I saw Katie on that sunny winter's afternoon in January when we played York City in the FA Cup. She looked so unbelievably beautiful.

I remember the Wednesday afternoon following the Bristol City game as we sat opposite each other in that cafe on Church Road in uncomfortable silence not knowing what to say to each other. I had an afternoon off work and Katie had finished her job at the bank as she was in the process of preparing to move.

"We certainly made a night of it on Saturday, didn't we, Katie!" I eventually said, unable to bear the silence any longer. Katie looked me in the eyes and smiled shyly.

Saturday had been complicated to say the least; after her friend Libby had joined us for a drink in the Prenton Park and once Sid had told everyone whether they wanted to know or not about what had apparently been happening between her from Mallory Road and the man with the mole from the off-licence, Katie had decided that she needed to go home and change for our night out. I remember being sat there in her apartment surrounded by boxes and bags, items going to friends, others to charities. Whilst her friend Libby was in the shower Katie would pace back and forward in very little, almost as if to try to tease me. Eventually my two female companions were ready, Katie clad in her famous blue denim miniskirt, and we headed for a night out.

It was a very tense atmosphere as I sat with Katie in this flash bar; her friend was flirting with some guy and I was left alone with my ex-girlfriend who I was still in love with wondering if a night out with her was really a good idea. We had another drink and finally started to talk; first about the Rovers, then about what we expected Sid to be doing and what he would be gossiping about in his given location, most likely it would be his new nemesis – her from the sandwich shop. Soon we got to the topic of the future; she said in an unconvincing manner how she was looking forward to her new beginning in Manchester with Jordan and that she was looking at getting a job in the centre of Manchester at a bank or financial-services firm. After wishing her all the best in an unconvincing manner I told Katie that I was on to something with the Polish lady who lived down the road from Sid and if it didn't happen I was considering moving to Canada. Also, Sid had told me that her with the red hair who teaches PE at the high school was a half rice, half chips type person and had a soft spot for me, too, so I might ask her out. When we looked at each other, we knew we weren't being honest with each other but we both declined to say anything honest and wished each other well in our proposed future endeavours. Something told me that Katie wanted to stay with me in Rock Ferry and that she knew I wanted her to stay with me in Rock Ferry.

When Libby announced that she had pulled the bloke she had been flirting with and was off to his place for a cup of coffee and the like, I decided it was time for a change of venue. I took Katie to a place called The Hideaway; it was a small nightclub in Birkenhead that I knew of. In the past I had frequented it regularly but not so much these days; it was hot and humid with plenty of misfits as patrons. It wasn't a typical nightclub pumping out tedious, monotonous dance music with a bar packed full of kids who were barely old enough to be in there and some who shouldn't have been in there at all. We got a drink and Katie headed to the dance floor; she signalled for me to join her but she knew that I wasn't a dancer. I headed to a pinball machine and fired countless pound coins into it, taking my frustration out on the machine. Every time I turned around I could see Katie dancing on the floor gazing into my direction as if she wanted me to join her. I would venture to the bar where I would buy a drink for me and one for her. She attempted to lure me out on to the dance floor but it failed. Countless men walked up to her and asked her to dance with them, she declined them all.

The thought of being so close to Katie but not being able to make a move drove me to despair. I stood at the bar with my back purposefully to the dance floor; a young woman walked up to the bar and started to hit on me. She was chatting me up, she wanted to know everything about me and wanted to do everything with me; eventually, I let her drag me to the dance floor. If looks could kill then the look on Katie's face would have sent her down for a long, long time. She slipped over, and after a few strongly worded whispers from Katie my female acquaintance slid away from the dance floor. Katie walked straight up to me and urged me to dance. I complied, I still couldn't say no to Katie. Suddenly, I found Katie's arms around me and mine were around hers; we found ourselves staring into each other's eyes and finally we gave into temptation. We kissed, it was amazing, and it was electric. For the rest of the night we didn't leave each other's arms.

Three o'clock in the morning rolled around and it was chucking out time. We didn't hail a taxi, we walked hand in hand back to Rock Ferry; we didn't talk much but we kissed a fair bit. We reached Katie's apartment around four o'clock and Katie simply led me in through her front door, into the bedroom where we made mad, passionate love. It was beautiful, so amazing all over again. It was like reliving the first night we had had together six months before. We continued to make love till around daybreak before we collapsed in an exhausted heap together on the bed.

We woke early afternoon; we said a few simple goodbyes a little while later. Katie explained she had to be out by five that afternoon and she told me that Jordan would be dropping around when he was back from London to pick her up. He wouldn't be impressed if he found me at her place of residence. I wondered what he would think if he found out I had slept with his girlfriend. Mind you, he wasn't one to talk. I enquired where Katie would be staying and she advised that she would be staying with Jordan for the next week. I asked her if she needed a hand with any of her stuff but she declined. Apparently, Jordan would have that all covered. Most likely a case of fly-tipping if I knew that creep; I could envisage all of Katie's belongings being dumped over the motorway. We made tentative plans to meet at the cafe on the Wednesday. To be honest I didn't expect her to show up. I had a feeling that I could be sat alone all afternoon like a complete fool. I was pleasantly surprised to be wrong though.

"How did it go with your Polish lady friend?" Katie asked.

"It didn't," I replied, awkwardly. "I asked her out, she declined, enough said! Plus she's had her hair cut really short and it makes her look a bit like a butch lesbian!"

Katie nodded, "You really deserve someone special, Tommy," she told me. "You're an amazing guy!"

I smiled wryly at her comments and avoided saying something sharp and sarcastic. "Do I really?" I asked, feeling extremely uncomfortable all of a sudden.

"I think you would like Vicky; she's a former neighbour of mine!" Katie informed me.

"I think I've met her," I answered with another wry smile, "bad teeth, crooked smile, big nose and not much between the ears."

"So, you aren't interested?" Katie enquired with a slight grin.

I laughed and shook my head. "No, I'm not!" I replied.

"Shame," Katie said to me, "she could be the one!"

"She's a horror bag!" I laughed.

It was then it struck me; I had a revelation and I came to a conclusion there and then. "Why do you keep trying to set me up with unsuitable women?" I asked Katie.

Katie shrugged. "I don't know!" she answered, "are they unsuitable?"

"First there was Kim," I began, "who you don't like and knew I wouldn't like," I added. "Then there was Libby who I had a disastrous date with in the past and now another horror."

"I just don't want to see you alone," Katie replied, weakly. "We may no longer be together but I still care about you."

"No, Katie!" I said softly, she looked me in the eyes. "You don't want to see me with anyone else because you want me to be alone. You are still in love with me, Katie, and you want me for yourself."

CHAPTER ELEVEN

The End of Rock Ferry's Greatest Love Affair?

On the weekend before she left Katie had a leaving party at the Sailing Club, again she booked karaoke, and again I had that horrible excruciating pain in my stomach. I really didn't want to be there but Sid and Jean dragged me there. Jean said it was important I was going to be there for Katie; Sid said it was an excuse to get trolleyed and I was to always remember Milton Keynes. It hurt when I laughed; it hurt when a toast was made to Jordan and Katie; it hurt when I wished her all the best. It hurt when I sang the Righteous Brothers and I could see that loving feeling in her eyes.

I splashed the water from the tap on to my face and sighed; I looked up at the washroom mirror before I dried the excess water from my face. I felt hot and uncomfortable so I thought maybe splashing some water on my face would help me feel fresher. As I stared into the mirror of the washroom at the Sailing Club I felt my temper fraying; I could hardly bear it. I had had words with Jordan, I knew he was trying to taunt me but I bit when I knew I shouldn't; I tried to regulate my breathing as I remembered my promise to myself about not throwing anymore punches. I had told him if he ever hurt Katie then I would really hurt him badly; I told him that I knew what he had done from the start and if I ever got the chance I would destroy him. I felt angry but not with him; I was angry with myself

I was so angry, deep down I knew Jordan wanted me to make a fatal error in Katie's presence; he knew as long as I was friends with Katie then his future with her was in jeopardy. Funny but I had initially viewed Jordan as being a bit stupid but he wasn't. He was cunning and manipulative; he knew that the way to sever

Katie's last ties with Rock Ferry was to eliminate me as a threat. If he could make me look bad by doing something reckless then it was all over. I would lose Katie for good and he would win, leaving Katie under his vile grip forever.

I recall how Sid was attempting in vain to explain to some poor unfortunate soul that the three football teams in the English football leagues with rude words in their names were Scunthorpe United, Arsenal and Manchester F-ing United to no avail when Jordan came over for a quiet word. He could see me gazing admiringly at Katie recalling our lovemaking the previous weekend and he knew it was time to strike. As I've said before scum have a sixth sense for knowing when to strike.

"You stay away from my property!" he warned me. "I know every drug dealer in town!" he continued. "We'll come down here and tear this place apart!" he added. "Then we'll tear you apart and then your house!" he further threatened. "You touch her and your dead!" he told me. "You're all dead!"

I tried not to pay any attention, these were just words, words can't hurt me, I thought. Then he began with the heavy stuff.

"I've got this job working as a minder for this guy in Manchester!" Jordan boasted. "He's one of the top drug dealers in Manchester. Once we get out there I'm going to pimp her out to all his clients. I'll make a fortune out of that slag!"

He had hit a nerve, he knew that I was still in love with Katie, it was so obvious that I was; he hit back once more with the news of something I had always expected. "Remember Lee McGurnigan?" he threatened. "I sorted you out for him! Clifton Park – he paid me two hundred quid to put that bottle in you! Do you know what? That was the best two hundred quid I ever earned!"

I sighed again as I stared into that mirror once more; the water had done no good, maybe a bit of fresh air would do the trick. I didn't want to let Katie see that Jordan had got to me, but more importantly I didn't want Jordan to see he had got to me.

Along the way that night I acquired another horrific admirer. I didn't know who she was or who she came with but she took a drunken shine to me. She kept asking me to buy her drinks to which I declined. She kept asking me to dance, once again I declined. I didn't like her; I told her straight that I didn't like her, nothing about being tired or having a sore back, I just told her. She wasn't attractive or a nice person; she was gobby, selfish, ignorant, shallow, overweight and sweaty plus she had an obnoxious grating voice; so naturally she went for me. Why do they always go for me? When she asked me for a quickie I felt so nauseous I had to slip out to get away from her.

There was a nice garden outside the Sailing Club; I found a quiet spot and sat down on a bench. The cool fresh air finally did me some good and my head began to clear slightly but all I could think of was my gorgeous Katie with that rotten thug. To refer to her as my Katie sounds a bit chauvinistic but she made me feel so complete, she really was The One. My time with her was the greatest time of my life: deep down I knew we were meant to be; deep down I knew I loved her; deep down I knew she still loved me. Why had we split over a stupid row? If I had been more honest with her would we still be together? But then again how do you tell a girl, "You know that rotten piece of scum ex-boyfriend of yours? I beat the living crap out of him a few years back; punctured his lungs and fractured his ribs!" and then when she shrieks at you hysterically to explain you tell her, "Do you know why? He tried to kill me! Some drug-dealing scum paid him to put a bottle into me!" Jordan knew how to play Katie; he just manipulated her back into his life for his own personal gratification. Jordan didn't care about Katie; he just got off on being able to control her.

After about ten minutes of sitting on the bench thinking of my soon to be lost love I heard a distinctive voice, very grating; it was my admirer! I fell off the bench mistakenly believing she had found me and wanted to indulge in a carnal act. I was about to slip off into the safety of the undergrowth when I heard another voice; she had found herself a victim and from the sound of it he was very willing; I didn't recognise his voice though, the accent sounded like it was from the Home Counties and the individual was explaining to the Troll that it was how they naturally spoke. I could hear them fondling and smooching, telling each other how great they were, how sexy and gorgeous each other was; I felt like telling them how nauseous I was. Soon they were well, having it off; very loudly. Why don't I just slip back inside, I thought, do myself a favour; that was until morbid curiosity got the better of me, kind of like when someone has thrown up after drinking too much and you have a bit of a look at it then quickly regret it or when you see some roadkill at the side of the road and have to have a peek before quickly regretting that, too. I peered through some bushes to the spot where the 'loving couple' were expressing their love for one another physically. I couldn't help but wonder who her willing victim was. My heart skipped a beat when I saw who her willing victim was; it was Jordan!

All I could think was 'How could he?!', that rotten vile piece of scum! He has the greatest girl in the world and he cheats on her? With that?! I had to tell Katie; she would be devastated. Then I thought, what happens if she doesn't believe me? She might think I'm trying to stir up trouble. I could look like the jealous ex and she might think I'm a knob; I just knew Jordan would manipulate the situation making me out to be a liar and turn Katie against me for what could be the final time. Then again one of my long-standing beliefs about Jordan was confirmed; his accent was, indeed, fake! I was tormented; I slipped off back to the club.

I tried to slip in quietly but the first person I saw was Katie, "Still here?" she asked with a smile.

"Yes," I said flustered, "I went outside for some fresh air."

Katie could see something was bothering me. "Are you

okay?" she asked with concern.

I looked at her, should I say something? "I've not been feeling particularly great," I told her, "a bit of a stomach pain."

Katie smiled kindly and sympathetically, "Go home if you want to!" she said to me, she hugged me.

"I'll be okay!" I replied. "I want to stay here for you!" I looked her in the eyes and she looked into mine, her lips looked so appealing and suddenly I found myself looking at her with the thought of 'should we?' That moment reminded me of that day when we had first met in January.

I regained my composure then lost it when I remembered what I had just witnessed so I went to the bar. Sid was at the bar chirping on about the time he did 'thing'; what thing is I've never found out but he did it once. I ordered a peppermint and soda to ease my stomach.

"What's up with you?" slurred Sid.

"I've got a dodgy gut!" I explained.

"Got the trots have you?" asked Sid, crudely.

"No!" I replied quickly. "I've just seen something unpleasant!"

"Jean's not got hold of some poor teenage lad on the dance floor and tried to take has pants off?" asked Sid with a laugh.

"No but I wish it was that simple!" I answered.

"What is it then?" Sid asked, his curiosity raised.

I whispered in his ear. A look of shock ran across Sid's face. "That piece of scum! How could he do that to Katie?! But how could he do it with that little sweaty troll woman?!" Sid exclaimed. "Just the thought of that wants me to lose my dinner, I'll need a pep and soda myself now! And I always thought his accent was fake!"

"I don't know how he could do that!" I murmured unhappily.

"You have to tell Katie!" Sid whispered.

"I can't!" I replied. "She might think I'm starting trouble!"

"What are you going to do?" asked a concerned Sid.

"Nothing," I told him. "You're going to tell her!"

"No, I can't!" exclaimed Sid. "She'll think I'm an interfering old woman!"

"No she won't, Sid!" I tried to tell him. "She would never think that!"

"She does! She already thinks I'm like an interfering old woman!" Sid told me. "You have to tell her! You're in love with her!"

"I can't tell her!" I advised Sid. "She'll think I'm a knob!"

"Bloody hell!" mumbled Sid and staggered off.

I ordered another peppermint and soda before I headed outside again. I sat down on a bench, I couldn't go home, and I really needed to speak to Katie. Not about Jordan and that tart; about me and her. I sat there running through what I would say in my head; this could be the last chance I could ever have with Katie. Suddenly I was aware of a presence, "Hi..." said a soft voice.

"Hello, Katie!" I said, nervously wondering about whether I would dare tell her how I saw how her delightful boyfriend had just cheated on her with pig-woman hybrid. No, I thought, I just wanted to talk about her and me. I had a big question to ask her.

She sat down next to me, we looked at each other. We said nothing and gazed into each other's eyes. She looked amazing, the way the moonlight shone on her eyes, the way a nearby light shined down on her hair. I just wanted to kiss her.

"Are you looking forward to Manchester?" I asked eventually as the tension became so unbearable.

"Oh yes!" she said with feigned enthusiasm.

"As long as it's what you really want and you'll be happy!" I said positively.

"Thank you," she said, unhappily. "Jordan and I are really looking forward to it!"

"Where is Jordan?" I asked curiously.

"He had to go home," she told me. "He wasn't too well apparently, and he was complaining that he had stomach pains!"

"Poor lad!" I said unsympathetically. "Who was that little fat sweaty woman?" I asked after a pause.

"No idea!" Katie replied. "Some little slapper who I didn't invite!"

I noted some venom in Katie's voice. "You don't like her, do you?" I said.

Katie scowled. "Not in the slightest!" she said with more venom. "She just strikes me as a complete bitch!"

I cuddled up to her. "I'm going to miss you!" I told her, deciding to steer the conversation into another direction.

"I'll miss you, too!" she replied, she rested her head on my shoulder.

"You look beautiful!" I said.

"Thanks!" she said, flattered.

I kissed her on the lips. She smiled. I kissed her again. She smiled. Then we gave in and kissed passionately. I ran my hands over her fantastic body, we broke from time to time and I reminded her how beautiful and amazing she was and most importantly how much I loved her.

Finally we stopped, "Are you really sure you want to go to Manchester?" I asked, my forehead resting against hers.

She looked at the ground, then sighed heavily and unhappily; she looked up and by the look in her eyes I knew the answer. "No..." she sighed eventually.

"Don't go then, Katie!" I said firmly.

"I said I would," she replied unhappily. "I gave my word!"

I looked on unhappily into her beautiful eyes. "Can I give you one last kiss then?" I asked.

"Yes!" she replied; she leant over and we kissed. Perfectly, just the right amount of lip pressure and tongue.

"How was that?" she asked.

"Magic!" I said, softly.

"I'm going to miss you..." she added. "Would you like to be very naughty with me?"

I didn't need to be asked twice, especially by Katie. She led me through the garden to a secluded spot. "This is the only place the security camera can't see!" she whispered as we kissed and groped in between uttering to each other how much we loved one another. I dropped to my knees; I can still remember her moans and groans of pleasure and the moment of intense pleasure and excitement.

I was still on my knees as Katie was adjusting her clothing; she was breathing heavily. "We should be heading back inside," she said eventually, "people might talk!" I was still on my knees. "Tommy, come on!" she said.

"I love you, Katie!" I whispered.

"And I love you, Tommy!" she replied.

I reached inside my top pocket; I moved on to one knee. "Will you marry me, Katie?" I asked presenting a ring. "I want to spend my life with you! I love you...Please stay..."

I looked up at her beautiful eyes, I could see the surprise and shock but I could also see the conflict. "I can't..." she said softly and sadly.

"Do you not love me?" I asked. "I know you want to stay in Rock Ferry with me! I know you don't want to piss off to Manchester with that piece of scum!"

"I do love you," she said. "But I'm leaving, I'm going to Manchester with Jordan to make a fresh start! I think I need a permanent break from Rock Ferry and you. I'm going to Manchester to get my life back on track!"

My heart sank.

Rock Ferry certainly is a strange place. Welsh songstress Duffy sang a song named *Rock Ferry* about moving here and building a house. She also recorded an album about this area of just under fourteen thousand people in Birkenhead which is part of the Metropolitan borough of the Wirral in the county of Merseyside but only since the local government reorganisation that took place on the 1st April 1974. I've lived here all my life;

I've never experienced life outside it in any form and for the first time in my life I was wondering whether I should leave Rock Ferry and spread my wings just like Katie was going to. The occasional trip away was all I knew of the world outside Birkenhead.

Katie's words earlier that evening after our liaison around the back of the Sailing Club had been a powerful body blow from which I was still reeling. Not only declining my proposal of marriage but telling me she wanted to get away from me and Rock Ferry was extremely painful. My heart had sunk when she told me she was going; my head had been in such as mess following the events of the previous week, I thought I was doing the right thing by asking for her hand in marriage. As I lay there in my bed unable to sleep, puffing away on a cigarette during the early hours of the Sunday morning before Katie was due to go, I began to think of my own mortality and future.

Maybe I should think of flapping my wings and moving away from the safety and security I had in Rock Ferry. Perhaps it was time I had a fresh start away from the monotonies of many broken hearts and Rock Ferry Tobacco Duty. I had seen adverts in the *Daily Star* stating that the Canadian Government were looking for qualified professional people to emigrate to the Great White North with the promise of earning thousands. I just had a vision of it all: I could move to Canada and gain work as a plumber where the frozen environment of Canada would freeze my broken heart so it wouldn't be damaged any further. Maybe I may find a fellow Tranmere fan out there and we could start a supporters club for exiled Tranmere fans in Canada and North America. Perhaps I could even give up smoking; what would be the point of paying Rock Ferry Tobacco Duty if I wasn't resident in Rock Ferry?

I puffed away on a cigarette as I desperately tried to analyse Katie's words; why did she want to get away from me and Rock Ferry? Why did we have that romantic liaison behind the yacht club? I understood her wanting a fresh start – but with Jordan? Please, that guy was a waste of space of the grade A1 variety. I hadn't told Katie that Jordan had been working at a fast food outlet known on a national level or of the words I had had with Jordan earlier that night or even what I knew had happened between him and Kim. The thoughts of the right hook that I would plant on Jordan's jaw danced through my mind but I knew that I couldn't force my luck on this; it could go one way or the other and most likely this would not go in my favour. I had proposed marriage and Katie had turned me down; she would think I was plain and simply just bitter. All I could think of was that Katie had conflicted feelings, which was why she wanted to get away from me. The going had got tough and Katie had decided to flee Rock Ferry. I was devastated.

The last hours of that party had been painful; I was unable to look Katie in the eyes. When I tried it was too painful and when I tried to speak to her I just felt rejection. Eventually the party concluded, we stole a few kisses when I walked her home and then we headed in different directions: Katie with her head held high destined for a supposed new life in Manchester the following day; and me, a plumber from Rock Ferry, off to Kirkfield Grove with a life ahead of me that consisted of ongoing heartbreak and handing out cigarettes to people I didn't know every Saturday afternoon before and after the Rovers had played. Whether I liked it or not, I guessed I would be an eternal slave to the phenomenon known as Rock Ferry Tobacco Duty.

I remember what I thought of as I lay there pining for my lost love; I just thought about what I would do if I ruled the world. If I ruled the world there would be a lot of things I would do. I would stop people from walking across the road whilst using a mobile phone. I hate mobile phones; they simply breed ignorance. I would ban mobile phones from public places. I have to go outside the pub for a smoke but when I come back in there is still somebody having a loud boring shouted conversation on a mobile phone that I have to put up with; unless I want go outside and freeze once more.

Another thing I would ban from public places is children; if people insist on owning them then they should keep control of them. My solution at supermarkets would be to place children in holding pens until their owners would be ready to retrieve them; I gathered that now The One was leaving my life having children wouldn't happen to me. I would ditch child benefits; people might take a bit of responsibility for their actions and the lives they create and I wouldn't have to pay tax to support benefit scroungers who don't want to work and preferred to live off benefits for their whole lives.

Nice girls would not be allowed to date, live with or marry tossers. Every man would be rated at the age of sixteen and every five years until it no longer worked downstairs or they had lost their marbles; if they were a tosser they could only date slappers, troll-human hybrids and attention-seeking mental cases. Nice girls would only be allowed to date, live with or marry men who would worship the ground they walked on and would treat them like the goddesses they truly were. Then I suppose that would be a breach of their human rights or some rubbish like that...

I would overhaul the Human Rights Act so that the rights of the victim would exceed the rights of the offender. When somebody would be sent to prison they would have to earn their rights and privileges. Persistent young offenders who were forever bleating on about respect would be sent to army boot camps to give them the well-deserved kick up the backside they required. Maybe they might be able to make a career for themselves and learn a little about respect.

I think I would get tough on professional footballers; I would take them to hospital for the day to tell show them what work is or send them out to help lifeboat crews for the day just to show them how easy their lives are. Then I began to think, what would I do if I ruled the game of football?

If I ruled football I would begin a series of overhauls that might let it retrieve its title of the beautiful game. I would bring in a wage cap for players; I can't justify the ridiculous amounts of money paid to the ungrateful prima donnas of the Premiership. I would bring in a wage budget to level the playing field; it would mean that the Multi-National Corporations would have to limit the amount of prima donnas they have on the field of play. If the prima donnas threatened to go abroad to get more money I would let them; the I expressions on their faces when no continental teams of any note wanted them would be priceless, as would the expressions of those who would come running back with their tails between their legs realising they were are not good enough.

I would bring in a transfer cap and bring in a transfer budget; how can a fee of over eight figures be placed on human beings? Is this no better than people trafficking? The smaller clubs would be able to compete in the transfer market; maybe the passions of the players would finally exceed their greed.

Cheats would be punished. Those who act like prima donnas and throw themselves on the floor to gain a penalty or free kick would be punished by video referrals and would be subject to suspensions. When they served a suspension they would have to wear a shirt bearing the notice of wimp to show they are a bit of a cheat. Or maybe this was a result of me just being a bit vindictive. I love my football but I just hate the BS that comes with it; the greed, the sleazy agents, glory hunters, hooligans and the control money has over the game...I suppose that when it comes down to it I don't hate That Bloody Stretford Mob that much, just the assorted BS that attaches itself to them...

CHAPTER TWELVE

Sunday Morning

Sunday mornin', praise the dawnin'
It's just a restless feelin' by my side
Early dawnin', Sunday mornin'
It's just the wasted years so close behind

Watch out, the world's behind you
There's always someone around you who will call
It's nothin' at all

Sunday mornin' and I'm fallin'
I've got a feelin' I don't want to know
Early dawnin', Sunday mornin'
It's all the streets you crossed, not so long ago

Watch out, the world's behind you
There's always someone around you who will call
It's nothin' at all

Watch out, the world's behind you
There's always someone around you who will call
It's nothin' at all

Sunday mornin'
Sunday mornin'
Sunday mornin'...

(C) 1967 – (Reed/Cale)

Sunday I just stayed in bed; I used to love Sunday morning, that day of the week where you didn't have to get out of bed if you didn't have to and want to. I also really loved the song of the same name by the Velvet Underground. I awoke and lay in bed for a few hours. I just didn't have the desire to get out of bed, I didn't want to get out, and I just thought what would be the point of getting out of bed? My one true love would be out of my life forever and I felt like a shell of a man. All I did was lie there in my bed remembering the good times I had with Katie at Prenton Park recalling the great Johnny King, the great times we had at New Brighton and the Albert Dock, the amazing days we had in bed together when we just didn't feel like doing anything else. I remembered the moment we shared the night before, the heartache when she declined to be my wife, the anger that she would be leaving to live with pure scum.

I felt like getting up and going around to where he lived and punching his lights out. I would tell him how he had the greatest girl in the world and he was a disgrace because of the way he treated her. He was nothing more than a snivelling, cowardly bully; the type who walks around like they are God's gift, that they are the big man, that they are a tough guy but in fact they confirm that behind every bully there is a coward. The previous night I walked her home to where she was staying with Jordan; we stole a few kisses before she went in. Katie had told me that she had to sleep on the couch; she had feebly tried to explain that Jordan only had a single bed into which two people couldn't fit. It didn't shock me; I could just imagine Katie as the mistreated wife of a bully who would kick her out of the bedroom so he could spend all night romping with some slut. If Jordan had a single bed then I must be a follower of a Premiership multinational corporation. Jordan made my blood boil; I always felt he was responsible for the end of my relationship with Katie; he set out to split us up, he knew Katie was happy with me and he couldn't accept it. I wished he would just drop off the face of the planet.

Eventually Dolly decided that I had to get out of bed and feed her. She sat on my pillow, meowing pathetically and batting me with her paw. After half an hour being fished at by a firm white paw, I dragged myself from my bed and fed her some rabbit cat food. Then I returned to bed; I had been slumped in bed a while when I decided to put a record on. It was a record Sid had given me, *Let the Heartaches Begin* by Long John Baldry. Sid had once been a close personal friend of a former close personal friend of the aforementioned Mr Baldry. He had given me the record a few years earlier when I had split from a girl under very unhappy circumstances, as is the way for me. He felt I was bottling up my emotions and needed to release them. I listened, I wept, it all flowed, and I felt somewhat better. I've always felt that I get love wrong; if I can get it wrong, then I'll get it wrong.

I must have listened to that record for three straight hours. I did nothing else; I just lay there listening to the song over and over again. My neighbours must have been tolerant people. That or they were away. I recalled the moment I split from Katie – did we really split up because of that argument? That stupid argument we had about that piece of drug-dealing scum? She thought I was a brute, but then I thought back to the previous night; she didn't think I was a brute then. My head was a mess. I just couldn't accept that she had picked him over me. My life suddenly seemed to have no purpose.

Monday came along, the day she was supposed to leave. I had one job to do. It was for this nosey old bag in Devonshire Park. I had some minor jobs to do around her house, she hung over me on every job questioning everything I did, wanting to know why that was necessary, that she understood I was a workman but was there a necessity to wear overalls, that they didn't do things like that in her day and whether there was really any need to do that. In between her expert opinions on plumbing and telling me how to do my job she began to talk about that awful football club, the noise that came from there, the horrible fans. She said she loathed the parasitic underclass who attended games and Margaret Thatcher should have crushed them when she had the chance. Football, she explained, was the reason we no longer had an empire, church attendances were down and why the death penalty should be restored. She commented on why it was a disgrace that a pastime such as football was called sport whilst a true sport and historical, cultural pastime such as fox hunting had been banned. The old bat explained that if she had the money she would buy that horrible football club and shut it down, then buy some private land where she would breed foxes and allow the rich and the landed gentry of England to hunt the foul beings to their hearts' content. She asked if I went to church and when I said no I thought she was going to have a fit. The old bag explained further that she'd had to get an electrician in and was horrified he was an Asian; she was even more insulted when he presented her with a bill. "How dare he!" she ranted, borderline hysterical. "If anything people like that should be paying me to allow them to make their presence in my home! It wasn't like that in the good old days when we had an empire!" I left a bill overcharging her and went home.

It was about 11 a.m. and I had nothing to do, nowhere to go. Following two minutes of pondering I picked up my iPod and walked down to Rock Ferry Pier. I took the ferry to Liverpool; I listened to *Ferry Across the Mersey* all the way, giving a menacing stare to those who looked down their noses at me. I walked around the Albert Dock and recalled the day out I had had with Katie there. I hopped on a bus and headed to Liverpool Cricket Ground. I gawped in for about half an hour; there must have been about six people who told me, "There's no cricket today!", at least ten people thought I had escaped from the local loony bin. I jumped on to the next bus and took the train from Garston Station to Hamilton Square then transferred to New Brighton. I enjoyed the funfair, had some ice cream then called some

Burberry ape a tosser just for the fun of it. I got back on the train and went to Ellesmere Port. The boat museum was shut. I headed up to Bromborough and had haddock and chips with lashings of salt and vinegar at the chippy. I told myself that weekend I would go down to Llangollen and ride the railway, just for old time's sake.

My last stop of the day was Clifton Park. I went to that road where it all began. I saw a glass bottle lying in the gutter; I picked it up and walked to where it had all happened. I paused for a minute or so; a rotten thought went through my head, but cooler thoughts prevailed. I threw the bottle in the nearest bin. I wasn't scum; I could never do that to someone, not even to any bullies and, I doubt, even to Jordan.

I got back to Rock Ferry about 8 o'clock; I stood for an hour on Bedford Avenue waiting for a smoker. Eventually a man wearing a Manchester City shirt waltzed along puffing on a cigarette; I walked towards him. "Alright?" I asked casually. "Who will City be playing Saturday?"

"Aston Villa!" he scowled. "It's a bit ignorant not knowing who one of the premiership's richest clubs is playing!"

"Sorry, support my local club!" I replied.

"You a blue noser or a red noser?" he asked.

"Neither," I replied, coolly. "I'm a Tranmere fan!"

"Just a loser then?" he smirked sarcastically.

"Got a spare cig?" I asked after a pause.

"Yeah..." he said as he passed one over.

"Spare one for later?" I asked, hopefully.

Somehow I got through my work on Tuesday. I was meticulous, not one error. I was polite and charged the going rate. I did one job straight after another, no breaks, no lunch, I started half eight and finished at half six. My mind didn't once veer towards my lost love, I wouldn't let it. But once I returned home it did. We were supposed to play Newcastle that night. I didn't want to go. Officially I said I was knackered but the unofficial truth was because Katie would not be there. It just didn't feel right without my gorgeous Katie; she was in Manchester with him! Okay there had been games where I went alone, but she was no longer in Birkenhead, our love seemed over; did this spell the end of me and the Rovers, too? Had Johnny King's magic finally worn off? Was it time for me to sell my soul to the Premiership and trade in a real football team for a soulless multinational corporation with fake fans, prawn sandwiches and other assorted BS that accompanied them?

I lay in bed again; I had a premonition that Tranmere were going to get a hiding that night; it would be the omen that finally signalled the end of my relationship with Katie. When I heard the rain on my window I felt justified. As the rain intensified it felt even more justified. The right decision had been made; it was warm and comfortable in my bed. I began to tell myself that one day I would eventually move on and love again; but would I ever be able to find a person who was as amazing as Katie was?

I couldn't settle so I switched on the radio in order to keep up with impending doom. Shortly after I switched it on Newcastle took the lead. I drifted off to sleep and as I awoke the news came through that Tranmere had won 2-1. I thought nothing of it; I'd probably misheard or dreamt it. I drifted off again. I fell into a troubled little sleep where I was being harassed by the authorities for a crime I had not committed.

A little while later I dreamt that there was somebody knocking at the door, a policeman with a warrant for a crime I simply could not have committed. When I awoke it was 10.15 p.m., and it wasn't a dream; I could hear someone knocking at the door. Suddenly it hit me. Tranmere had won! I leapt out of bed and headed downstairs, it was with great trepidation that I approached the front door; I unlocked the door and then opened it...

"Hi..." said Katie with a smile, she was soaked through.

"Hi, Katie!" I said trying to remain calm. My heart was

pounding, I was so surprised to see her; could she be ready to step back into my life so soon? "Come in," I told her, "you're soaked!"

I got her a towel and she dried her lovely long hair. She had been to the game; I'd have loved it apparently. Michael Ricketts scored two late goals after the Geordies had led for 74 minutes. The Newcastle manager had been red-carded. For once, for one strange instance I couldn't have cared less about the Tranmere game, there were more important matters I cared about.

"Why aren't you in Manchester?" I eventually asked; it still hadn't quite sunk in that Katie was suddenly and rather amazingly back in my life.

"I was sat on the train at Liverpool Station with Jordan," Katie began, "he started to tell me about his new job; he would be a minder for a drugs baron, he was also involved in extortion rackets and people trafficking – I was going to be a prostitute for this revolting man." I could see a tear in her eye, I hugged her. "So I said I needed the ladies and then I slipped off; I left him, I found the courage to walk away. I came back – I went to the game...and I realised...I wanted to be with someone who loved and appreciated me, someone who cared...someone who makes me feel happy!"

"So why did you come to me then?" I asked with a grin.

"Because I love you!" she replied. She smiled and we locked lips. "Do you know he fly-tipped all my belongings over the motorway last week?" Katie added.

I cuddle up to her. "Where are you staying?" I asked.

"With Jean," Katie replied. "Jordan doesn't know where she lives so I will be safe. I tried dropping round yesterday."

"I was out..." I answered.

"I noticed," Katie replied. "Where did you go?" she asked.

"I just went here and there!" I told her.

"Good for you!" Katie replied with a beautiful smile, her expression changed. "Why didn't you tell me about Jordan and that pig-faced woman on Saturday?"

"How did you know?" I asked.

"I saw the security camera footage," she told me. "That's why I found our quiet spot; why didn't you tell me, Tommy?"

"I was scared you wouldn't believe me!" I admitted.

"I would have believed you," Katie smiled. "It would have made things easier and I just wanted you to be honest!"

I cuddled up close to Katie. "Would you like to move in with me?" I asked.

"Like I should have the first time?" she asked rhetorically.

"You'll be safe here," I reassured her, "he can't hurt you when you are with me! You know Jordan was working at a fast food outlet and not a fancy restaurant?" I added.

Katie smiled sadly and nodded. "Yes, I saw him there one afternoon," she began, "he got fired for having sex on the job with this big, fat, rude girl who knows that bitch Kim!"

"He's never going to hurt you again!" I reassured her, wrapping my arm around her gently.

We kissed again, she looked into my eyes. "Sid told me everything about the bottling and Saturday; I should never have believed Jordan, that man is such a bastard! You gave him exactly what he deserved! Do you know he spent all Saturday night shagging some other slag whilst I lay on the couch listening to them?"

"So would you like to move in with me?" I questioned again, moving the subject on quickly.

"Only if you'll marry me!" she smiled beautifully. "I realised that I didn't need to get away from Rock Ferry after all and I certainly didn't need to get away from the man I love..."

Epilogue

I've been married to Katie for just over a year now, we had a small ceremony at a registry office and held the reception at Dixie's. Katie finally got to meet my family and, surprisingly, they got along, even my elder sister got along with her which was a total shock. We went to the doctor's a few weeks ago; Katie is now six weeks pregnant and we are now preparing for the clatter of tiny football boots. If Katie has a little boy she's still keen on the first name Robert but he will definitely have the middle names John King at my insistence.

Last year whilst we were on honeymoon in the Lake District I wrote to our hero, Johnny King. I thanked him for bringing me together with Katie through the mighty Tranmere Rovers. I told him of the brilliant memories we had shared because of his involvement at the team. Johnny King was the greatest, I told him, and if anyone deserved a stand named after them at Prenton Park, it was him. I finally thanked him for being such a major influence on my life and the two most important things in my life, Tranmere Rovers and my lovely, beautiful wife.

A week or so later, Mr King replied. He thanked me for my letter; he said it was always nice to receive fan mail even in your twilight years. He was flattered by our appreciation and simple fan appreciation can do far more than any accolade ever will. Mr King said it was nice that I'd found love with Katie but he could never take the credit for bringing myself and Katie together. That was fate. He said our tale was a heartening story; it was a tribute to the club and to the fans. He added that it showed that sometimes football could mean more than what actually happens on the pitch. He wished us all the best for the future.

Neither Katie nor myself has regretted marriage, we mean so much to each other. Although we are happy together there has been some sadness. My close friend James William McConnell better known as Sid is no longer with us. Whilst walking home about five months ago he was set upon by a homophobic gang, they beat and kicked him mercilessly then ran off leaving him for dead just because he had an alternative lifestyle. He died of his injuries a few days later in hospital. They were not football fans or even football hooligans, just a group of pathetic yobs so insecure with themselves and who were so threatened by the presence of a fifty-something-year-old gay man that they decided to attack him. Both Katie and I miss him tremendously. Sid once gave me a piece of very valuable advice: you have to be honest with yourself before anybody else, Sid had struggled for most of his life with his sexuality and he said the hardest person to tell who he was gay was himself. He was my best man at my wedding. Jean was maid of honour.

Jean has found herself a new gentleman friend by the name of Wilf; they met at our engagement party at the yacht club and went on their first date to the Albert Dock. Dolly has been recently placed on a diet; she's gained a bit of weight since there are two people around the house to share meals with and there are two people to lie between on the bed. Katie is eating for two now so Dolly looks on pathetically during mealtimes hoping fruitlessly for a little something but has been told it's for her own good.

Susan has acquired a toy boy and brought him to meet us both a few months ago; suddenly she has given up the notion that I could do with an older woman and accepts Katie is the one for me. Cousin Aubrey was unable to attend my wedding because he was preparing for his own civil union to a former boy band member that took place a few months ago; I returned his compliment by not turning up to his civil union as he didn't attend mine. That, plus I wasn't invited, well, except for my younger sister none of my side of the family was invited, so there was no real loss there. So there's nothing new there.

My younger sister has been sharing bath water once more and

she should be due around the same time as Katie; she's joining us for antenatal classes and it's nice my relationship with her is finally developing. I never knew how fond she was of Sid until he had passed on. Apparently she loved to gossip with him as well as enjoying his anecdotes. My elder sister is no longer dating her National Front boyfriend and has been very vocal about marriage. She doesn't think it's a necessity in this day and age and that people who do it are stupid and foolish as well as being so emotionally insecure that they feel they have to commit to someone through a pointless ceremony that was money orientated. I just think she is being a bit moody and jealous, she wasn't the centre of attention and her brat wasn't asked to be a bridesmaid. I read in the paper a few months ago that my ex, Hannah, had been sent to prison as a terrorist; in one of her left-wing loony moments she had taken up the cause of extremists and tried to side with them. It appears he got all too enthusiastic and the constabulary ended up with so much evidence against her that she won't be experiencing freedom for a while.

I can also confirm that I have not thrown one single punch since I vowed for Katie's sake not too. News filtered through to us a few weeks after our wedding that Jordan had been sent to prison. He was arrested for his part in the murder of a man who refused to let his business be used as a front for a drug-dealing operation. When Katie first moved in with me we took out an exclusion order keeping that nasty piece of work at distance should he return; I didn't want him to get near Katie. He had not been back to Birkenhead since he left and hopefully, now he's inside, he never will. With any luck he'll be in prison for a long time and can never cause my beloved wife any further harm and distress. I must admit that I've drank a toast or two that may he rot in prison for years to come. I also received news that Lee McGurnigan was now no more but that's another tale for another day.

Tranmere ran out of steam that season when I got back

together with Katie. We stayed in the second tier of English football and have now settled into the position of mid-table stalwarts. It's still the ultimate love affair to support Birkenhead's finest, the pleasure and pain, elation and frustration, the triumph and heartbreak. Katie and I have always felt there were three in our relationship. There was me, my true love Katie and a club once managed by the legend that it Johnny King.

A new man has taken over at the pub up the road by the station. He's from Hereford and is very much a non-local, a lot of the stuck-up old brigade have gone and lot of normal people have started going back to the pub. I went there last week with my friends and had one of the best nights out I'd ever had. It just goes to show that a change can be as good as a break. The thoughts I had of going to Canada have now receded as I never wanted to stay in Rock Ferry so much in my whole life.

With a baby on the way I've had to make a few savings and tobacco was one thing that had to go. It was a bit of a struggle to begin with but Katie says it smells nicer around the house and I'm saving a bit of money. My health seems to be better, too. I no longer have to go and freeze outside the pub if I need to have a smoke in winter, which is an added bonus. But probably the strangest phenomenon is that now when I get stopped on Bedford Avenue on my way to Prenton Park to watch Tranmere Rovers I am no longer eligible to pay Rock Ferry Tobacco Duty.

Roundfire Books put simply, publish great stories. Whether it's literary or popular, a gentle tale or a pulsating thriller, the connecting theme in all Roundfire fiction titles is that once you pick them up you won't want to put them down.